World of a spy

—a jungle of savage, silent death and betrayal—
peopled by men and women like

Steve—the "insurance man" traveling under orders
from East Berlin . . . and somewhere else

Armour—who knew too much for a government lawyer

Janni—the kind of girl men always love—and always
leave

Feather—a devastating dancer—and deadly hostess.

This is the nightmare world of

THE DAVIDIAN REPORT

"Practically any tale to which Dorothy Hughes has
set her hands has, by my records, been lively coursing.
This seems to be one of the best."

—James Sandoe, *New York Herald Tribune*

The Davidian Report

DOROTHY B. HUGHES

WILDSIDE PRESS

THE DAVIDIAN REPORT

For my son,

Antony Allen Hughes,

with my thanks for his help in preparing this story

I

THE GIRL HAD BOARDED the plane at Kansas City. She wasn't a girl he would have noticed particularly on the street or in a crowded room. He wouldn't have given any especial attention to her in an empty room, or on this plane, if she hadn't taken the seat beside him. There were other unoccupied places—no window seats, it was true, but plenty on the aisle. All right, she had to sit beside someone and she'd selected him. Maybe he looked harmless. Actually she'd not given the impression that she'd seem him at all. It was rather that she'd decided to select the third row left up front.

She was medium size and yellow-haired, her dark green suit was a tweed import; her felt hat was shaped like a riding hat, the kind society girls affect to appear country; and her suede pumps were the exact color of the darker weft of the tweed. Her purse was large, of good black leather, well rubbed; she protected it against her in the seat. It was big enough to be a formidable barrier between her and a seatmate. She kept her hands gloved, yellow crochet gloves, and she used a five-cent yellow pencil on her book of crossword puzzles. It was a long time since he'd seen anyone as devoted to a crossword puzzle as was this girl.

Her face was shadowed in the miniscule overhead shaft of light invented for plane travel, but he had photographed it with his memory on initial appearance. A small chiseled face, a cold little face, but that might have been put on like her horn-rim glasses to preserve her privacy while traveling. The crossword-puzzle book could have been for the same purpose.

He knew the detail of each other face on the plane as well as hers. Not only the passengers remaining, but also those who had left the plane at Kansas City and at Albuquerque, including the thin-faced man, jockey size, who had been his seatmate preceding the girl. Most of them were, by his figuring, safe. The dubious ones he went

7

over in his mind until he would recall a scrap of elbow, a hunch of shoulder, an ear tip, no matter how or where he met it again. Despite the most careful planning, it was never possible to say that the Feds didn't know about a job. They were like the wind, invisible, but able to penetrate the impenetrable room.

It was one reason for his insistence on playing a lone hand. Only because he'd had good luck in carrying through a couple of his initial errands did he get anywhere with the insistence, and because his friends had managed to mess up one of his simplest jobs with their nursemaids. He couldn't be certain that they hadn't set someone to follow him, despite the hell he'd raised the last time that was pulled on him. He could never be certain they weren't having him watched. The bossman was an old woman about a man on a man ad infinitum. No imagination, no scope. But he was the bossman.

He wasn't sure of the young soldier, crumpled asleep in the right aisle rear seat. In front of the pretty, competent hostess, a safe one, with her bright painted-on smile. What was a gawky boy with not so young eyes, wearing a government issue, ill-fitting uniform, doing on board the Constellation from New York? He looked as if he should be thumbing a truck on the highway. And there was the beefy character with the brown hat pulled over his hatchet eyes. Midsection right. Another, Albuquerque on, a withy man, who kept turning discreet attention to the tweed girl.

And the front section right, New York these, a team with bulging briefcases resting against their ankles. The one by the window was a small sandy man in horn-rims. The aisle one was a big fellow, his features handsome in a big vivid face, his well-cut dark hair carrying just the right flair of gray for current glamour. His gray suit was of rich material and rich tailoring. He had a rich voice to match. He could be a big-shot lawyer, the kind you were able to retain for a basic fee of ten thousand per annum. His hands were big and square and clean as the rest of him; he smoked an indefatigable cigarette.

Steve Wintress didn't know why he was particularly uneasy about this one. Maybe the man was too much the sure-of-himself success guy. Maybe because the fellow had tried to strike up a conversation at the Albuquerque break. Not that this should have appeared suspicious. After flying together across the continent, after excusing themselves at the previous stop for trying to be the first off into the

8

smell of fresh air after cold, stale altitude, it wasn't out of line to speak a friendly word. But if the guy was looking for conversation, why didn't he talk to Junior next to him? They'd scarcely exchanged a sentence during the flight.

There was something wrong with the picture, although as yet Steve hadn't figured it. The man couldn't be on his side, he was too assured for that, too lacking in furtivity. Yet he could scarcely be a Federal and for near the same reasons; the Feds went in for quietness, anonymity. To be sure, there was no telling what either side had dreamed up to make sure of this deal. The Davidian report was too important not to take bold steps to win.

The plane was losing altitude, floating down out of empty darkness to behold the glitter of red and green and yellow lights, flung out like a fabulous jeweled scarf. Phoenix. Next stop L. A. The usual warning glowed against the forecabin's door, cigarettes were stubbed out in the midget ash containers, the pretty hostess made her customary competent double check on seat belts.

Steve didn't have to climb across the tweed girl, she was in the aisle on landing. Nor did he try to jockey the big man for second place, the Albuquerque approach still stuck in his craw. He waited until the aisle was moving before joining the tail end of it. As he passed the crumpled soldier, the boy blinked sleep-grained eyes and closed them again in disinterest.

Outside, the desert heat of the day lingered in the stillness. The stars were bright and sharp as pins. The usual scattering of men and women who, at all suburban airports, watched the plane come in, were there, leaning against the wire fence, sizing up each passenger as if they'd never seen a stranger before. The passengers headed for the lunchroom or to stretch their legs in a stroll along the portal. Steve walked as far as the portal but the big man was too much in evidence there. His voice, if not his words, came reverberating along the walk. Steve walked back to the grass plot for his cigarette, standing in the half-shadow of a dusty tree, smelling the good, hot air.

On the field the big, yellow oil-service trucks were diminished to miniature under the giant Connie wings. The soldier boy emerged from the plane; he was small as a toy, high in the open doorway. The green tweed girl came along the path from wherever she'd disappeared to. As she passed, her eyes met Steve's. Hers flicked away at once; she was discomfited that she'd turned her head to see who was standing there, more so that it had been he. Steve grinned. It was the first moment of relaxation he'd allowed himself in four days.

The twenty minutes were brief. The passengers began trailing early towards the gate, just as if they believed the plane would take off on the dot. They knew better. Steve dropped his cigarette stub to the grass and brought up the rear. He remained well to himself crossing the open field. He was hoisting himself up the uncomfortably steep steps of the ladder when he remembered that he hadn't seen the big man. Against his will—out of curiosity, not nerves— he checked over his shoulder. The man was only now striding through the gate, stopping just inside it to exchange words with the attendants. They were six-footers but the man topped them.

Steve continued up the ladder, ducked his head and re-entered the plane. As he proceeded forward along the narrow aisle he checked the passengers automatically, unobtrusively. The hatchet face and three others had disembarked for good at Phoenix. There were three new ones, all women, teachers, smartly dressed, off to a special meeting on the Coast. They unfurled snatches of bright talk a little too loudly, excited in journey's beginning.

The big man didn't plunge down into his seat until just before the take-off. As he clipped his seat belt, he addressed his companion: "L. A.'s fogged in, Timothy." His voice was strong enough to carry through the plane. "It'll be Palmdale or Palm Springs." Whatever else he had to impart was lost in the rabbit rustle of the other passengers. And also because, as if realizing he'd created a commotion, or satisfied that he had, he was content to speak down.

The hostess tried to answer the bubble of questions with the panacea of the professional smile. "We don't know yet. It's possible we may be able to land at Los Angeles. Or Burbank." The pretense soothed some of the protestants. "I'll let you know as soon as the captain has word."

Steve didn't ask any questions. In late November you could expect fog on the Coast. He didn't like this disruption of schedule. He'd given himself a week, including flying time, to take care of the Davidian business. It was overestimation; with any luck at all, it wouldn't take three days. He wasn't superstitious, but a bad break at the start of a job was bad luck. Not that he was worried about missing Albion. Albie would be waiting at the airport what-

10

ever time Steve put in. But whatever plans had been made for a meeting tonight wouldn't come off.

The girl put away her book and removed her horn-rimmed glasses. She didn't like this either. Steve spoke to her. Not like a guy trying to get acquainted but like a disgruntled traveler. "Where's Palmdale? I know Palm Springs but where's Palmdale?"

She turned to him and he saw her eyes for the first time without the protective coating of glass. They were too big for her face. Just now they reflected the green of her suit; they were colored like a cat's eyes and were as unwavering.

"I don't know exactly." Her voice was without coloration. "North, I think. In the desert."

He waited a proper moment before asking offhand, "Your first trip out?" as if it were also his first.

"No. I live in California." She was disturbed but not at him. "I wonder what time we'll get in. If they'd told us about this in Phoenix—"

"They never tell the passengers anything," he replied. "They're worse grannies than medicos for keeping the populace ignorant." He eyed her. "You being met?"

She shook her head briefly to discourage questioning. He wasn't discouraged. He went right on talking, as if he were one of those guys who never caught on to a brush-off.

"I am. I was," he amended ruefully. "How long the guy'll wait, I don't know." Albion would wait until hell froze over. But it sounded more human this way.

She murmured vaguely, "We'll be so late . . . an imposition . . ." She ended the conversation there, snipping off her light beam, settling herself for sleep.

He didn't push it further. He too settled himself, although he had no intention of dulling his wits with sleep, or any particular need of it. He was a night man.

It wasn't too long before the hostess went forward. Now they'd have it. She returned almost at once, put on the top lights, and took her stand for a speech. As charming as if she were bringing good news. Not the information that they were landing at some Godforsaken hole where busses would be sent to carry the passengers to the International Airport. Everyone came awake and full of questions. Yes, their luggage would go along with them. Yes, there was a telephone in Palmdale and there'd be time to put in a call. It was the tweed girl who asked that one; someone was

11

expecting her if not meeting her. The hostess parried, she was gentle and bright, and she got away as soon as possible, leaving the passengers friends in misfortune, not seatmates by accident.

The girl said, "She said telephone, singular." Her narrow shoulders gestured: And all of these people!

"I noticed she said there'd be time. How much time?"

The man behind them leaned over Steve's chair. He was all right, his wife was with him, they were returning from a district Kiwanis convention. "Don't worry about time. It takes hours to dig up those old crates they send out to Palmdale. Stuffing out of the seats, broken springs, no heat—I said the last time I'd stick to the Chief."

The ones who hadn't been through it before were more resigned. The three young teachers of Phoenix were rather titillated over the unusual. The big man across the aisle actually appeared pleased over the development.

The pilot put the ship down in Palmdale only a little later than it should have landed in L. A. There was no scarf of jewels to guide him, only endless open space, forlorn pylons, and a barracks-like shack. The stars were as bright as in Arizona but the air was chill, sending everyone hurrying to the shack.

It shouldn't have surprised Steve to walk into hustle-bustle. Theirs wasn't the only ship set down at this isolated way station; all other lines had been closed out by fog as well. But somehow you didn't expect a desert barracks to be milling with people in the late night. Balancing the confusion was the apathy of those who had been waiting far too long. They huddled beneath their coats on the rackety wicker couches and scuffed chairs. A handful of luckier ones encircled a big iron stove borrowed from an old-fashioned steel engraving.

Most of Steve's plane headed for the wooden counter where two farm women were selling coffee and cold, thick sandwiches. A sparser line formed outside the telephone booth. His girl hadn't been first, someone was already in the booth. She was next, the big man behind her. They were talking in desultory fashion, in the way a man wouldn't miss a chance to talk to an attractive young girl. Not that she was particularly pretty, certainly not now, her face pale and troubled, but compared to the other females in the shack, she was a *Vogue* model. Steve's gabardine when new hadn't resembled the one draped across the shoulders of the big man.

12

Steve edged to the outskirts of the food counter. He wasn't hungry; however, the stimulus of coffee would help pass the time. And from this vantage point, he could spot who had cared enough to be first in the phone booth. He was vaguely surprised when the crumpled soldier emerged. Although it was logical; the boy had been in a position to be first off the plane. If he had taken advantage of the last minute of leave, as kids would, he'd need to put in a call quick. The soldier shoved his cap over his other ear and dug his hands into his pockets as he neared the counter. It gave him a more shabby look. The hands-in-pockets gesture evidently wasn't an idle one. He was veering away when Steve got his eye.

"Buy you a coffee, kid." He knew how to say it with just the right rough edge to take off any smarm of charity. He'd worn a uniform himself not enough years ago. "If we can get near enough to buy one."

The kid said, "I'll help push." His sudden grin was more young than his face. The smile went into his eyes and they too were young. It might have been that all he had needed was the transcontinental sleep.

There was an entering wedge behind the sandy man. As Steve moved, he jogged the briefcase under the man's arm, but it was the sandy man who apologized, "Sorry." He balanced two cups of coffee, one for the boss, out of the way. The soldier nailed the spot.

The farm woman's voice was harsh. "Coffee? Beef or ham?"

Steve said, "Two coffees. Beef or ham, soldier?"

"Beef, I guess."

The boy was thin and kids were always hungry. "One of each," Steve said. While they waited he heard the girl's voice.

"Could you get me a cup of coffee?" She was holding a quarter over his shoulder.

He didn't take the coin. "Sure," he said, and, "Make it three," to the gaunt woman. He swiveled his head. "Did you get your call through?"

The girl said, "Yes." No more.

The soldier picked up the paper plate of sandwiches and one of the coffees. Steve paid and took up the other cups. "Now if we can find a place to park ourselves."

They were lucky on it. The busses for an earlier plane were coming in, hostesses were passing the word to their charges. The soldier was quick at snagging the couch with

13

the broken springs. It wasn't comfortable but there was room for three. They put the girl between them and passed the sandwiches.

She said, "I'm not hungry."

"Eat it. Good for you." The boy was taking a big hunk in his mouth but he managed the young grin. Surprisingly she reacted, half-smiling back at him. It made her look human, not like a pale green schoolgirl in tweeds.

Steve handed his sandwich back to the soldier. The kid was near ready for another. From under his eyes, Steve was watching the big man, over there by the stove. The man was watching the three of them or one of the three. It wasn't possible to know which way it was. When he started suddenly in their direction, Steve returned his attention to his own group. "At this time of night I stick to coffee."

There was time for no more before they were towered over. The big fellow said, "I got through, Miss Talle. The car's on its way. May I offer you a lift to town?"

Steve was faintly surprised that the man knew her name, they hadn't appeared to know each other on the plane. And she was evidently chary of giving it, there'd been no introductions between the three of them collaborating on this sprung couch over their late supper.

The man explained to Steve and the soldier, "When I heard in Phoenix about weather conditions, I wired ahead to have a car sent out." He laughed, "I've ridden the bus from Palmdale before." The invitation was proffered easily, no pressure, "If you men would like to ride along—"

The soldier accepted without hesitation. "Sure. Thanks."

Steve wasn't so sure. He'd like to know how this guy could find out where they'd be landing before the hostess knew. Possibly Mr. Big had ordered a car to proceed to all possible points. Even while he hesitated, Steve was telling himself it couldn't be a trap. The man and the girl and the soldier coudn't all be together on this, to prevent Steve Wintress from reaching Davidian. To excuse his hesitation, he said, "I'd have to go to the airport anyway."

The man stepped on his words. "Any place you like." His smile was almost as professional as that of the air-line hostess. "I'm Haig Armour." He tossed it out as if he expected them to know the name.

Steve's eye didn't waver. Haig Armour, attorney with the Justice Department. Haig Armour, former big noise of the F.B.I. Steve had heard enough about Haig Armour, but

14

he'd never run into the man before. He didn't know if to-night was an open move or accidental. Mildly he returned, "My name is Wintress. Steve Wintress."

If Armour recognized the name, he didn't admit it.

The soldier said, "Private first class Reuben St. Clair. Call me Rube." His smile was comic relief.

Armour set down his briefcase and reached into the pocket of his handsome weatherproof. "How about a little heat for that coffee?" He pulled out a leather-encased flask. "Brandy." It was out of character that he didn't give the Napoleonic date.

The girl said, "No thanks," and the private refused, "Afraid it might put me to sleep."

It could have been drugged and the three working together. But it didn't smell like anything but the best brandy. It was what Steve needed. He said, "Thanks. I was just wishing I had a drink."

Armour's assistant was coming across from the doorway with quick little steps. Steve began to drink his coffee. The sandy man had a sandy voice. "The car is here, Haig."

"Fine." Armour shared his smile with the three. "You ready?"

"You bet." Pfc. St. Clair pushed up on his long legs. He carried his sandwich with him.

Steve went on drinking the coffee. They wouldn't leave without him.

Armour took the Talle girl's cup and helped her to her feet. "You tell the hostess we're off, Tim. We'll want our bags." He remembered. "Timothy Leonard, Miss Talle, Steve Wintress, Reuben St. Clair." The name Leonard wasn't familiar to Steve. "These kids are going to ride in with us."

Steve didn't qualify as a kid but maybe he looked it to Armour. Or maybe Armour was considering Steve's stature, not the lines in his face. He drained his cup before joining the parade led by Haig to the door. He'd taken it too fast. he felt a little giddy. And again he wondered if the lacing could have been tainted, if the oddly matched trio actually were linked. The first blast of night air helped him to clarity. And standing around in the cold while the reluctant attendant unearthed their bags from the jumble helped more. There was nothing out of character in the luggage; the girl had expensive matched stuff, excess weight; Armour's was as expensive and as heavy. Rube carried only a small khaki bag as shabby as his uniform; Timothy

15

Leonard's suitcase was unobtrusive. Steve retrieved his worn valise.

It was Timothy who directed them to an oversized black limousine, bigger than a hearse. But it was Haig who arranged the seating, stowing the soldier up front by the shadowy driver, relegating Timothy to an anachronistic jump seat, and deftly spotting Steve in the rear between himself and the girl. It might be accidental, but Armour knew how to fence in a man.

2

Steve fought sleep. It was essential he reach the airport and not some destination Haig Armour might prefer. But the brandy had been heavy and taken too fast. He knew he'd slept when the boom of Armour's voice shook him into consciousness.

The big man was leaning towards the driver's shoulder. He'd pushed aside the glass panel separating the tonneau from the cab. "My God, Wilton, how can you see anything?"

The machine was creeping through gray fur. They were on some planet where there was no light, no shadow, no presence, nothing but the shell in which they were encased, and the amber beams of their fog lights bending into the engulfing fog. The driver undertoned something without taking his eyes from the windshield.

Reuben commented cheerfully over his shoulder, "You can't see nothing. Nothing at all."

After a moment Haig decided to leave it up to the driver. He shoved the dividing partition tight and settled back again into the upholstery. "He said we're at Sherman Oaks. How can he tell!" He passed his cigarette case. Steve alone accepted; the girl might have been asleep.

"I've got to go to the airport," Steve reminded him. He had no idea of its direction. He took a light. "But you can let me off at any taxi stand."

"Nonsense," Haig refused heartily. "On a night like this? Private St. Clair wants to go to the airport too." He leaned across Steve, raised his voice. "What's your destination, Miss Talle?"

She turned her head slowly. Her eyes were blurred with sleep. "Benedict Canyon. In Beverly Hills." The yellow-gloved hands pressed together.

Timothy Leonard said, "Haig and I are stopping at the Beverly Hills Hotel. The same neighborhood."

"You don't mind riding first to the airport?" Haig said. It wasn't a question; it was the way it was going to be.

Steve protested uselessly, "Rube and I could hop a cab along the way. It would save you the trip." He knew before he spoke that Haig Armour had made up his mind on this before they left Palmdale. It was almost as if he knew that Albion was waiting for Steve Wintress and that it was a meeting he intended to witness. Let him. He'd see two old friends say hello, no more than that. Steve gave up. Actually at two in the morning in this pea-souper, a cab might be hard to materialize.

As they crept through Sepulveda Canyon, without reason the fog thinned out into tattered veils. They could see the dark walls of the pass, the white guardrails, even glimpse white stars in the overhead sky. And with no more reason, as they emerged into Westwood at the opposite end of the canyon, the night reverted to another furry density. Again they crawled tortuously along the highway. But there was some evidence of life here, a neon-decorated, all-night garage, the occasional glisten of pale headlights. It was long to the airport; Haig Armour hadn't realized how far out of the way it was. He was silently restive, his face against his window. The Talle girl seemed to be sleeping again. Timothy slept. Up front Rube St. Clair was gabbing with the driver, but the glass partition withheld their words.

They reached the airport at last, turning off in pale fog by the large blinking green arrow, following the road to the in-turn, past the empty acres reserved for parking, up to the curb in front of the terminal. Armour swung out of the car first. It was courteous, and the man's long legs must need a stretch after this run. But Steve wasn't happy about it; he wasn't taking any nursemaid into the terminal with him. He didn't want more trouble. This had been as ill-met a night as he'd had in years, he couldn't take any more.

Reuben was on the walk; he began to make his manners while the driver was bringing Steve's valise and the soldier's khaki bag from the trunk.

"Don't mention it," Armour pushed aside the appreciation. "You boys find out if your friends are around. If not, come back and ride in with me. I'll wait."

Steve's fist tightened on the valise handle. But he managed to speak quietly, even pleasantly to the bastard. "Don't wait. We'll be all right from here on in. Thanks for the

17

lift." He walked away fast, the soldier on his heels. They separated inside the door, without any word, each on his own errand.

The terminal was as crowded as the desert shack had been, with those dogged friends and relatives who wouldn't give up. The loud-speaker rasped endlessly, "Flight Nine arriving by bus from Palmdale. Pick up your baggage at the street entrance. Flight Fifty-nine arriving—"

Albion wasn't in the milling crowd, wasn't leaning on the ticket counters or on the newsstand. Steve began a slow pace past the chairs. Each one was occupied by a stranger. The phone booths were empty. He went into the men's room, this too was empty. It didn't add up. Albion would not have left the air terminal until Steve got there, no matter what the hour. Unless something had gone wrong earlier and Albie hadn't come at all. But that didn't add up either. There'd have been a substitute. Albie was thorough.

Steve covered the room again, as if he could have missed Albie on the first count. He wasn't there on the second either. While he was knuckling his brains, his conscious eye beheld the two doors leading to the court in the rear. He strode to the nearest, the one on the right, and pushed out into the fine fog. Albion must have ducked out here for some reason, possibly because he'd spotted something off color within. Something Steve couldn't be expected to recognize; he hadn't met the California boys.

There were no shapes in the fog, no one on the bench just outside the door, no one leaning over the fence looking out to the blurred landing field. Steve walked over to peer down the empty ramp. No one. Nothing. Turning back, he saw what he had missed before. Across the court on a smaller bench, there was someone or something, a darker mass against the fogged dark. For a moment he was motionless, conscious only of sounds, his breath and the dripping of fog from the roof. Then he moved quickly, quietly. It was Albion, hunched there in his worn raincoat, a shapeless, colorless hat pulled over his eyebrows. He might have been asleep, but his knees were placed together too neatly, his hands crossed over them in peace. Steve didn't touch him. He tilted the man's hat brim with one careful finger, but he had known before that. He walked away, returning to the lighted, busy terminal by the far door.

No one seemed to notice his re-entrance. He lit a cigarette, steadying it with cold fingers. The immediate move was to get a cab into Hollywood. He was heading for the street exit

18

when the soldier emerged from Men's. Reuben's face had grown old again from fatigue or disappointment. From both. He said, "Your friends not wait either?"

"Looks like they didn't," Steve admitted. He couldn't have been as long outside as it seemed. Unless the kid had been told to wait for him.

Reuben walked along towards the door. "You don't suppose that Armour guy'll still be hanging around?" It was a wishful query.

"No," Steve said. Although he wasn't sure of the soldier, he offered, "I'm getting a cab. You can ride along with me to Hollywood if it'll do you any good."

Reuben was appreciative. "I'm heading that way."

And then they saw the big car, the rear door still wide, Haig Armour emerging from the tonneau. "No luck?" Armour's voice implied that he'd known there wouldn't be. "You two must have taken the place apart, nail by nail." He'd changed the seating, he had Timothy by the driver and he himself took the jump seat. The girl slept on in her corner. She didn't stir when Reuben shoved beside her, making room for Steve. But if you touched her she wouldn't topple; she was breathing.

"And now?" Armour asked.

"We'll get off in Beverly Hills." Steve settled his valise under his heels.

"Where are you going?" There was a hint of impatience in the big voice and Steve wanted to answer it straight: *None of your God-damn business!* But he said, "Hollywood. We'll take a cab from Beverly Hills. I'm sure Miss Talle isn't up to any more side trips."

"Yes." Armour agreed too readily. "You can drop us and then Wilton will take you two wherever you want." He blocked Steve's protest. "It's a hired car."

Steve shut his mouth. Rube was already accepting in his lackadaisical fashion, "Well, thanks, Mr. Armour. Someday I'll give you a lift."

Fatigue silenced all of them. The fog ebbed and flowed about the car through Westwood and into Beverly Hills. They turned away from the city on a broad avenue sentineled with giant palms, slender and tall as Watusis. The fronds were lost in the dark white mists overhead.

The driver held speed to a walk. The avenue was sparsely lit, the intersections lost in the fog. Again theirs seemed the only vehicle in motion, themselves the only living organisms in a vanished world. The Beverly Hills Hotel was a beacon, its yellow lights penetrating the gray. The car didn't hesitate at the hotel. For a moment anger seized Steve. And then he realized from the growing darkness that they were moving into Benedict Canyon. The climb was tortoise slow, the driver pulling under far-spaced and dim street lights to decipher the street signs.

The girl said, "I don't know where we are." It was the first thing she'd said since leaving the airport.

Haig Armour didn't sound too sure. "Wilton will find it. You know your aunt's place?"

"I can't see a thing." Her yellow-crocheted forefinger rubbed against the window as if she could make a hole in the density.

One estate was like another on the Benedict Canyon road, shrubs and trees, the mass of big houses fading into the white shadows. Wilton was out of the car, turning a flashlight on a country-style white mailbox, lettered in black. And he was again in the car, heading further up the Canyon. It wasn't more than a long city block before he repeated the routine, this time returning to open the rear door.

"This is it, Miss Talle." He didn't talk like a chauffeur, there was a quiet authority in his voice.

Miss Talle said, "Good night." She didn't say thank you, possibly she'd said it before, or was too sleepy to care. Armour helped her out of the car, Wilton carried her expensive luggage through the gate. She stumbled after the man. He could have driven closer to the house; the iron gates of the drive were closed for the night but he could have opened them. Steve wondered.

Haig Armour took the place she'd vacated. It shoved the soldier closer to Steve, Armour was bulkier than the slip of a girl. Through a yawn, he commented, "Her uncle is Eldon Moritz."

The name was nothing to Steve. Or to Reuben.

"She dances. Ballet."

It meant no more than that Haig Armour had asked her a few questions while they'd waited at the airport.

Rube asked, "Is she in the movies?"

"She's been in a couple. Just background motion."

Steve asked, "What does her uncle do?" If the name meant something to Armour, it wouldn't hurt him to know.

"He's a director," Armour said.

Wilton's steps crunched on the gravel. He came out of the fog, climbed under the wheel without a word. He somehow managed to turn the car in the narrow lane and it crawled down the long winding hill again to the lighted oasis of the hotel. End of the run for Haig Armour and Timothy Leonard. Armour tried once more. "You boys want to put up here for the night? I can take care of you."

Steve spoke up before Reuben could get in an acceptance. "Thanks. I've got to check into Hollywood."

If the private was disappointed, he didn't let on. "I guess I better find my outfit before they think I'm lost. I'll go on in with Steve."

They repeated their thanks, watched Armour's confidence climb the broad steps to the hotel porch, the silent Leonard at his heels. A uniformed attendant appeared for the luggage. And Wilton was suddenly standing at the car door, looking in.

Steve said, "You can drop me at the Roosevelt." Reuben didn't say anything.

The fog held, now faint, now furry, along Sunset and the Strip into Hollywood, turning over La Brea to the boulevard. Both Steve and Rube swung out at the tall lighted hotel. They had their bags in hand, there was no reason for the man to leave the wheel. Reuben said, "Thanks for the ride." Steve added, "Thanks." He gave a half salute. You wouldn't be expected to tip Armour's driver, and besides, he wasn't a driver.

Steve stood there on the walk until the car had pulled away, filing in his memory what he had seen of the man. Not a hired driver. Plain-clothes cop? Federal Bureau? Haig Armour wouldn't be in town on an unimportant assignment. No one could say with certainty that Armour had actually left the F.B.I. Certainly he'd been prosecuting Justice cases, he was a lawyer, wasn't he? Weren't they all who had joined in Armour's generation. But it could be a cover-up for more secret Bureau work.   ....

Reuben was eyeing the big hotel dubiously. "You going to stay here?"

Steve didn't like the way he was sticking, yet it needn't mean anything. It could be the kid didn't know his way around town and didn't have much coin. "No. I'm heading for a flea-bag up the street. I didn't think His Worship had to know." It wouldn't hurt to offer. "You can bunk with me tonight."

Rube spoke quickly. "I'm not broke. I didn't want any more handouts from Mr. Armour. Next thing he'd be winning the war single-handed." He crimped the grin. "It's

21

too late tonight to start looking for the guys I was supposed to meet—"

"I said you could bunk with me," Steve repeated. It was too brusque. He softened it. "I already won one war. I don't want any more medals."

The hotel he was heading for was past Highland, half-way between the Roosevelt and the Drake. An easy walk even with the valise to carry. There didn't seem to be any big black car cruising the empty street. Rube had another dubious eye when they came abreast the Balboa.

Steve reassured him. "It's a flea-bag. But Hollywood style." The lobby was small and fancy, glassed like a conservatory. It had enough red leather banquettes to set up a cocktail lounge. "A friend recommended it." Albion had said it was convenient.

The desk clerk asked no questions, only the rent in advance of registration. He was a blenched old man, his sparse hair dyed a ruddy brown. Steve paid, handed over his valise to the soldier. The key he put in his pocket; let the hop pick up a duplicate.

He said, "I got to make a phone call before I turn in." He walked past the phone booths out of the hotel.

3

He remained slantwise on the pavement outside until he saw Reuben disappear behind the elevator doors. He headed south then to Selma street. He'd memorized the location from Albion's notes. Even this near to Hollywood Boulevard, there were yet relics of a gentler day, old frame houses of the era of front porches and wisteria vines. These patches too would go; but they weren't shabby yet, they were well-kept, lived-in homes.

The fog was lifting with the early dawn; it was past four by his watch. He peered for numbers; he was on the wrong side of the street but he did not cross until he had found the house he sought. It was not as kempt as its neighbors, its gray paint was thinned by time. There was an old wooden swing and an old wicker rocker on the porch. The vines were without leaf this near to December.

No lights showed within, no shadow stirred behind the old-fashioned stiff lace curtains masking the front window. Steve climbed the three wooden steps of the porch without sound. He stood silently before the front door, not wanting to start this. After a moment his finger touched, barely touched, the bell.

He waited, his hands dug into the pockets of his coat, his hat half covering his eyes. At this hour a faint bell might not awaken a household long asleep. But he waited, reluctant to ring again, and the door came open. He couldn't see the man inside. A deep voice was overlaid with old European accent and suspicion. "What is it that you want?"

He answered, "Mr. Oriole."

The door was pulled wider, evidently as an invitation to enter. Steve walked in. He was in a small gloomy hall, papered in mottled wine color, cramped with an oversized oak hall tree, a chest to match, and a two-shelf bookcase. By a side window there was a worn leather armchair, eternally holding the sag of a large man, and a scuffed oak table strewn with newspapers. Above on the wall was a telephone with a coin box. A staircase climbed behind the chair, carpeted in the same worn green as the hall, the same color as the limp brocade drapery separating this room from what would be a parlor on the left. The staircase turned at a landing, hiding the upper floor. Directly forward where the hall narrowed into a corridor, another limp curtain covered another room. The only light on was a dim bulb hanging in the corridor.

The man was as shabby as the room. Flabby flesh drooped on his large stooped frame, on his shapeless face. He was half bald, the lank hair over his ears and neck a dirty gray-brown; his small dark eyes were both wary and uncurious. He wore gray trousers, shapeless as elephant shanks, a wrinkled shirt without collar or tie, and old felt bedroom slippers over his brown cotton socks. He probably hadn't been to bed, only snatched a laydown while waiting for Steve to report.

Steve questioned, "Mr. Oriole?"

"I am Mr. Oriole."

"Steve Wintress." He didn't take his hands out of his pockets.

Mr. Oriole began plaintively, "Where have you been? I have for hours been expecting you—"

Steve interrupted, "Trying to get here." He demanded roughly, "Where the hell is Albion?"

"He did not meet you?"

"He did not meet me," Steve parroted. He knew how to deal with stationmasters like Oriole. Jump them before they could start on you. "No one met me."

23

Mr. Oriole spoke with concern. "Mr. Albion was there. He telephoned to inform me the plane would be late."

"Maybe he got tired waiting."

"Not Mr. Albion," said Mr. Oriole.

Not Albie, never Albie. He took orders with a bulldog grip. Efficient, trustworthy Albion. Steve wondered which side had killed him. Not why, only who. He said, "I've got to see him. He has my plans."

"I will telephone to him," Mr. Oriole said. Not with confidence.

Steve sat down on the oak chest, pushed back his hat, lit a cigarette. He needed a prop. Mr. Oriole put a coin into the hall phone and dialed a number. The sustained ringing sounded faint and metallic in the quiet. Mr. Oriole waited a long time before he hung up. The coin clacked down the chute, he retrieved it and put it in his pocket before turning. "There is no response."

"Where does he live? I'll drop around there." This was the point to make quickly. Stationmasters didn't like giving out an address.

Mr. Oriole was no amateur to be stampeded. He pried into Steve's face. "You want a room?"

"I have a room. I want to see Albion."

"I will send him to you. Where is your room?"

"Balboa Hotel. If you haven't his address, I'll take his phone number." When the man was hesitant, Steve asked, "What's the matter? Don't you want me to see him?" That would throw a delayed scare into the flab when he read the afternoon papers. The news wouldn't make the a. m.'s.

Reluctantly Oriole divulged the number. He didn't like doing it; it was his business to get people together, not arrange for them to make contacts on their own. He eyed the scrap of paper on which Steve had written the information as if he would snatch it from his hands. Steve tucked it into an inner pocket. "Don't worry. I won't hand it to the F.B.I."

Oriole tried for a laugh but it wouldn't come.

"And don't call me at the hotel. I have a roommate."

At Oriole's startled grunt, Steve smiled insolently. "You don't know me, Mr. Oriole. Wintress is the name, Steve Wintress. They send for me when there's a special job to do. And I do it my way." He rubbed out his cigarette on the heel of his shoe, pitched the butt towards the table before he crossed to the door. "If you find Albie, tell him I'm in a hurry to get back to Berlin." He slammed the door after him, not caring how many he woke in that musty house. He didn't like armchair slobs giving him directions.

The morning was pale as he walked back to Hollywood Boulevard. No one followed him. It was easy to be sure because as yet the day of the city hadn't begun, he was alone on the side street, near alone on the blocks he covered returning to the hotel. In the hotel he passed the desk without a nod, passed the maroon uniform of the Philippine boy into the elevator. He had to look at his key to know the floor. "Fourth."

He used the key to enter his room. Reuben's breathing was even in sleep. Steve didn't need a light to undress; he dropped his clothes on the armchair, yanked the window drapes across the narrow gray windows to shut out the coming of daylight. At the clatter of the metal rings over the rod, the soldier raised his head. His voice was druggish. "Get your call made?"

Steve said, "Yeah. Don't wake me in the morning."

It would have been easy to thump the pillow over coming problems, but he didn't. He needed sleep; he would sleep. Whoever killed Albie wasn't going to run away, he'd be around to see how Steve was liking it. Because there was only one reason why a smart guy like Albion would have dropped dead at the International Airport last night. One reason only, to keep him from meeting with Stefan Winterich.

It was after eleven when Steve awoke, not a long enough sleep, but more than he could hope for again for the duration of this job. He glanced towards the opposite bed. Reuben was still embedded in blankets, his spiky brown hair rising like pins from the pincushion of the pillow. Steve propped to an elbow to regard the sky through the ragged line between the curtains. It showed gray.

His movement stirred Rube. The boy creased his eyes. "What time is it?"

"About eleven-twenty. Time to get on the job." He lifted the phone from the table between the beds.

Rube reached out for a cigarette. "You here on a job?" It was the first personal question he'd asked.

Steve said, "A little insurance investigation deal." He had the right credentials for it, too, in case anyone got too nosy. It was the kind of job that gave a man a legitimate excuse to poke around in varied neighborhoods. He'd memorized Oriole's coin-box number last night. He gave it to the

25

switchboard, said "Call me," and added, "Send up some coffee and stuff. Wintress, four-ninety." He told Rube, "We'll have breakfast this morning on the boss." A man needed a bit of coddling now and again. He lit a cigarette himself and pushed the pillows behind his shoulders.

Reuben said, "I ought to get going and see if I can find those guys. One of them has an aunt lives in an apartment on North Cahuenga. We were going to bunk with her."

"You on leave?"

"Yeah. I'm being reassigned. I just got back from two years in Berlin."

Steve's face didn't say anything; his face was trained. Berlin. And the phone rang. He slurred into it, "Who's speaking?"

The voice said, "Mr. Oriole." It was the right voice.

"Wintress. What's the news?"

Oriole had had it. He begged, "You must come here at once."

"What for?"

"It is not something to speak over the telephone. Mr. Schmidt is waiting for you. You will come." It was half question, half command.

Steve wanted to laugh. Here the name was Schmidt. It wasn't so much the news putting the tremolo in Oriole, it was a man called Schmidt. He said, "Soon as I get dressed and catch a bite of breakfast," and waited for the hysteria. He wasn't disappointed.

"You must not wait for these things!"

"I'd look pretty funny running around Hollywood without my pants. See you." He hung up, yawned a grimace. But he got out of bed. "I'll go ahead and shower. If breakfast shows up, don't wait for me."

"Sure," Rube said. He appeared young and disinterested lying there in bed. And he'd just come back from Berlin. He said for reassignment.

Steve didn't waste time in the shower, but Rube was swallowing coffee when he emerged. The smell was good. "Pour me some, kid. I'll shave while I'm eating." He plugged in his razor. Rube carried the coffee and a plate of ham and eggs to the bureau. "Should think you'd be spending your leave with your folks."

"What for?"

"Usual thing, isn't it?"

"Uh-uh," Rube said. "My old lady's got a new boy friend. She didn't want me around cramping her style."

26

"She can't be so old," Steve commented. "Your pop?"

"He took a walk twelve years ago."

"Where'd you live if you lived there?"

"New York."

"I was born there." Yeah, he'd been a New York kid once himself. A long time ago. He detached the razor and began to put on his pants. They could stand a press. He had a couple of clean shirts and a neat tie with little pink birds on an elongated navy sky, a girl had sent it to him for Christmas. He wore the plain maroon one. The shine on his shoes was still good enough with a rub-up. "Look," he said, "no use carrying your kit around all day. Bring your pals back with you around five and I'll buy the dinner." Big-hearted Steve. But he'd feel better if he made certain that there were pals before the soldier moved out.

"Well, thanks." Reuben was in character this early.

Steve caught up his coat, put on his hat, ducked back in to grab his room key and stow it in his pocket. He kept it there when passing the desk. No sense in advertising your comings and goings to strangers. There was a new man on the desk, a tall, thin, younger one, with a face like a sea gull.

It was as gray as fog out. Steve covered the few blocks to Oriole's steadily but without undue speed. Let them wait. He pushed hard on the doorbell this morning. There'd been a flutter behind the starched lace when he climbed the steps.

Mr. Oriole's face was wobbly. He hadn't washed, hadn't changed his clothes. "Come in, Mr. Wintress, come in."

Deliberately Steve delayed. "What's up?"

The flabby hand pointed towards the parlor. The green hangings were pulled apart, just enough for a narrow man to pass through. "Come in. Mr. Schmidt is waiting."

There was always a Smith or a Schmidt or a Smithsky. This one was a precise middle-aged man, wearing a banker's blue suit and a conservative tie of blue on navy blue stripes. His black shoes were small and high-polished, his fingernails dull-polished. His rimless glasses had no expression.

Mr. Oriole said, "This is Steve Wintress, Mr. Schmidt."

Schmidt said, "I've heard much of you, Mr. Wintress." He shook hands like a man in a countinghouse. There was no warmth in his voice. It could have been a tape recording.

27

Steve inclined his head. The parlor was small and hadn't been redecorated since the house was built. It was golden oak and green plush, as crowded with furniture as the hall. A luxuriant fern sprayed green fronds from a table by the front window. Steve took the straight chair by the side window, leaving the plush one for Schmidt; the light for Schmidt's face, for Steve's back. He asked again, "What's up?"

Schmidt said, "Albion is dead." His hand tightened imperceptibly on the newspaper he was holding. Early edition of the p. m.'s.

Steve reached for it. Schmidt had to lean far out of his chair to pass over the paper. It was a trick Steve had learned too long ago to remember where. To make the other fellow subservient. The story was a small one near the foot of the front page. "The body of Frederick Grasse—" that had been Albion's name—"was found early this morning," and so on. Officialdom believed that Grasse, feeling unwell, stepped outside the terminal for fresh air. Heart attack.

Steve read it word for word. He handed back the paper, again letting Schmidt come out of the chair for it. He propelled the question, "Who killed him?"

Mr. Oriole twisted his dirty hands. Schmidt said, "You believe he was killed?" His voice was dry as a pod.

"I don't think he dropped dead so he couldn't meet me." Steve came out of the chair and began pacing the square of old carpet. It could make guys like Schmidt and guys like Oriole nervous. "It wasn't the Feds—"

Schmidt interrupted virulently. "The F.B.I.! Cossacks! Tools of the capitalist dictators—" He was primed to go on with the well-worn speech but Steve cut him off.

"Don't tell me. Write your congressman." He walked over to Schmidt and stood above him, making him lift up his glassy eyes. "It wasn't the Feds. They take us alive. They want talk, not dead men. Who killed Albie?"

Schmidt said rigidly, "We will find out."

"Okay. And while you're finding out, what do I do? Play the ponies?" He walked back to the gushing fern. "Albion was carrying the information I need for this job. I've got to have that dope."

"You will have it." Schmidt eyed Mr. Oriole.

"By tomorrow morning."

Oriole's mouth drooped. "It is impossible!" At the warning of Schmidt's face, he explained hurriedly, "Mr. Albion worked for long weeks. We do not know how many places

28

he visited, how many persons with whom he spoke." The excuses were not being accepted. He swallowed hard. "It will be difficult."

Steve was brusque. It was either that or weep with the guy. "You think we're the only ones after the Davidian report? Who came in on my plane last night? Haig Armour."

"He is no longer with the F.B.I." Schmidt was full of knowledge. "He is here on another matter."

"Says who? What's big enough for him out here but Davidian? I've got to have that dope tomorrow."

Schmidt said thinly to Oriole. "Put everyone available on it."

Steve relented. "Make it noon. That gives you twenty-four hours." And that gave him twenty-four hours.

There were gaps which only Albie's knowledge could fill. Oriole and his research squad would never close all of them. Albion was too smart not to withhold some keys. Because in this racket you didn't know whom you could trust or for how long. But Steve was ahead of all of them; he'd been in on the Davidian business a lot longer than a couple of weeks. He'd been in at the very beginning, in Berlin. Which was nobody's business but his own, certainly no business of this puny West Coast outfit. In twenty-four hours he might not need Albion's material. Meanwhile, looking for it would keep the Schmidt crowd occupied.

He went back to the chair and gathered his coat; he hadn't removed his hat. "Noon," he repeated.

Schmidt came up on his small polished feet. "May I give you a lift?"

"I need exercise," he said ungraciously. He added to it, "I've got some thinking to do. If Mr. Oriole can't get me that material—"

"He will," Schmidt assured him, and "Oh yes, I will," Oriole quavered.

Steve completed his sentence, "—I'll have to do a bit of scratching around."

You couldn't say that Mr. Schmidt appeared alarmed, but neither was he complacent. His minions didn't scratch around, you could bet; as they followed procedure. He pattered after Steve to the swinging draperies. "It is true that you knew Davidian in Berlin?"

Steve gave him courteous attention. Even a neat little Continental half-bow.

"It is absolutely true," he said.

29

II

HE TOOK HIS TIME walking back to Hollywood Boulevard.
Not much of a boulevard, none of the elegance either of the
old-trees variety or of glassy modern towers. The one big
hotel and the one big department store were at opposite
ends of the main stem; westward the boulevard dwindled
into a residential section, eastward it moved on downtown.
There were a couple of big movie houses like delusions of
grandeur scattered along the way. But mostly the street was
home-towny, an overgrown Main Street. It was probably
why Hollywood Boulevard had become a lodestone. Any
American, except perhaps a born New Yorker, would feel
at home on it.

Large red trolleys clattered through the center lane, small
yellow busses stumbled against traffic. Vintage cars and an
occasional better one crowded the curbs; endless little shops
and movie houses and cafés backed up either side of the
sidewalks. And endless men and women and kids sauntered
on the treadmill pavement. The pace wasn't that of a city,
it was California easy. The shop windows were decorated
for Christmas shopping, heavy on the red and green and
pocket-size cellophane trees dusted with stars. The street
was decked out in the same spirit. Great green metallic
trees grew from the sidewalks, giant tinsel stars and bells
dangled overhead.

Steve hadn't been followed from Oriole's. He couldn't
be sure that he wasn't picked up on Hollywood Boulevard.
He was conspicuous in his hat and gabardine. The grayness
of sky didn't matter to these people; they didn't wear hats,
men or women, and the only coats were on older women.
After this morning, Steve was certain that Schmidt would
decide to put a dog at his heels. Schmidt didn't go in for
unorthodoxy. It was possible that he might be deterred by
orders to let Steve Wintress alone, but this depended on how
strong New York had made them. You couldn't count on

30

Smithsky not to promise one thing and perform the diametric opposite.

Steve knew where to start without Albion's findings. He alone knew where Davidian had first holed up in Los Angeles, he hoped the knowledge remained his alone. He had intended to bypass the seven-month-old trail, it had been Albion's job to bridge those months. But it was all he had now.

He accepted the off chance that a dog was already at his heels. Better to smell him out and elude him now rather than attempt it in the heavier traffic of downtown L. A. He walked towards his hotel leisurely, but he kept his eye peeled for an approaching trolley. He timed it to double back and be the last man on board. Two stout women and a soiled youth in a school jacket had boarded ahead of him. They appeared harmless enough. At the next stop it was women and kids. He checked a half dozen stops and checked off these passengers at various points along the boulevard. Not one of those he'd noted was left on board when the car clattered through the tunnel into the subway terminal.

The ride had been an hour long, a typical ride to the downtown area of a city, the shops growing more shabby in neighborhoods left behind as the crocodile metropolis crawled westward. The only off-beat sights were the dirty white round of once-glittering Angelus Temple, and a small lagoon with swans rising out of the placid water.

It was after two when Steve came out of the terminal into the crowded downtown streets. This far from the ocean the overcast was thinned, the sky created an illusion of a watery sun. His coat was a burden. He knew the city well enough, he'd had plenty of leaves here in the old war, the one to end war. He walked the half block to Fifth, turned the corner and moved on up to the corner of Olive. The park called Pershing Square was boarded up, behind a wooden fence excavators had plowed up what once had been the refuge of old men and pigeons.

From caution out of experience, Steve didn't continue directly to Bunker Hill. He stopped first in a small drugstore across from the Biltmore Hotel and shut himself into a phone booth. He faked a call, waited what seemed long enough. No one had come into the store after him, no one was loitering outside when he left the booth and continued his climb up the hill. This had been an elegant part of town. What remained was beyond pride or even remembrance of

31

the past. The dull smear of cement covered where once there had been flowering lawns and the benediction of trees.

Unlike its sister back streets of New York, this one was near to deserted. No housewives squabbled amiably as they rocked their baby carriages; no children ran under heels into the traffic. There was no traffic, not even a passing car. Nor was there curiosity evinced in a stranger, and he well knew a stranger was as recognizable in this isolated sort of community as on a village green. And as little welcomed. One thing was definite. He had not been trailed; he was alone on the block.

He found the number he was seeking, a big broad house, three fine stories of once-white frame, standing on a high-cut back terrace. There was a wide porch where the family would have rocked on a summer's night, looking out upon the quiet hills beyond. When the house was young. A flight of run-over cement steps led to the top of the terrace, a cracked cement walk to the house. He climbed sagging wooden steps to the porch and crossed to the front door. No one appeared to challenge the intruder. The knob turned loosely under his hand and he entered the murky hall. There were defiantly closed doors on either side of a large center staircase. A pay phone against the wall reiterated a nervous jangle. He didn't linger below, but began to climb the footworn stairs. Somewhere a baby wailed, somewhere a radio sang about a lovesick girl, somewhere a man and woman quarreled in short ugly spats.

On the second floor he walked a length of more closed doors, noisome and silent, and continued on up the back staircase. Three F was on third, the poorest location, without light from front or rear. He rapped on the dirty wood. When there was no response, he rapped again more sharply. He heard the loud outthrust of a door from the floor below, a man yelling perdition at a shrilling woman. The man's heavy shoes clattered down the stairs. And Steve rapped a third time, hard, under cover of the confusion.

The door came open an ell. In the aperture there was a segment of an old face, wrinkled past recognition. Only the kerchief wound about the head gave indication that the face belonged to a woman. The eyes were black and small as black buttons. And malevolent. The mouth spat, "Nah."

Steve put his shoulder against the door before it could close. He didn't expect her to understand, but he said, "I am looking for a friend."

"Nah," she repeated.

32

She pushed at the door but he was stronger. "I know that he lived here."

She muttered an unintelligible stream of sound. And from within he heard a sharp command in what appeared the same tongue. It could have been Czech. The order must have been to admit him because her grudging hand opened the door. Not wide enough to walk through but he could sidle inside.

It was a rather large room, it might have been the nursery in those older, gentler days. But it was diminished by dirt and time, by the big brass bed, and the stove and rusted sink, the cretonne-covered wardrobe, the oversized round table and motley chairs. There was a narrow window against the far wall, in front of it in a teetering rocker an old man wheezed in his sleep.

These things Steve saw, but only in suspended memory. For there was only one thing he knew he was seeing, the girl who had spoken the command. She was sitting upright on the tumbled cot against the farther wall, her short dark hair tattered about her face. She was wrapped in a kimono of purple cotton with giant pink chrysanthemums blooming over it. Her bare feet curled under the purple hem. Her hair was sleepy but her eyes were as big as the old woman's were small, and were as black and hard. He had never dreamed of finding her here. The one person he would not seek; the one person he didn't ever want to lay eyes on again. It was Janni.

His voice was as hard as her eyes. Only by keeping it so did he dare speak. "What are you doing here?"

"Did you think I should be in Beverly Hills or maybe Bel Air?" She held the kimono tight across chrysanthemum breasts.

He was without an answer, afraid lest he cry out to her, more afraid lest he move towards her.

She demanded, "What is it you want?" She loosed one hand, pushed it through her hair in the old familiar gesture.

Because he didn't know what to say, he asked stupidly, "You were asleep?"

"I work nights."

At the sudden anger that flared into his face, she laughed out loud. "You think you will find me in the cinema? The new Marlene Dietrich perhaps?" She laughed again, that short brutal laugh. "Yes. I am with the cinema. At nights I sell tickets on Main Street. It is a fine job."

He too could be brutal, to hide his relief and his agony. He said, "I'm looking for Davidian."

The mockery went out of her. The old lady hardened in the background, the old man slept on. Janni said, "He is not here."

"Where is he?"

"I do not know."

"He was here."

She flamed, "Haven't you made enough trouble for him? For all of us? Get out and leave us alone."

He didn't move. "I'm looking for Davidian."

"You think we have hidden him?" Her voice burned. "Look under the bed. Look in the stove. Look in Grandfather's pants. Look! He is not here."

"I know he is not here," he said distinctly. "But I know he was here. Where did he go when he moved on?"

Her mouth was insolent. "If I knew I would not tell you. But I do not know. When he went away, I told him I must not know. Because of such as you."

"Her?" His shoulder gestured to the old woman.

"She knows nothing. Not even her name."

"If you see him, will you tell him I am looking for him?"

Her eyes hated with cold, bleak hate. "Why should I? To send him running again?"

He forced it on her, from across the room. "Will you tell him that?"

She shrugged and she tightened the cheap kimono about her. Beneath it there was nothing but her body, the curves and planes that came alive in a man's hands.

"Tell him that. Let him know. It's better for him to know."

She gave no response at all, only the width of her blank, black eyes. He didn't know what she would do. She would decide. He turned on his heel. The old woman had the door open for him. There was a curse on her blanched lips.

He wasn't noiseless leaving the house; he defied its ugliness. At the front door he paused briefly before stepping out into the city. If a tail had caught up with him, it wasn't visible. He went on down the hill to Pershing Square. He rode the trolley back to Hollywood, to his hotel. Blanking the memories from his mind, mocking at desire. A street girl; maybe she was selling movie tickets on Main Street and maybe she wasn't. Maybe she was singing the little song again, dancing the dance. She had been fifteen when

34

they first met, five—six years ago. He'd been too old for her then; he was too much older now.

Reuben was stretched out on the bed, perusing the comic strips in the evening news. He said, "What do you think? We're asked to a cocktail party."

"Who?"

"Feather Talle. She'd called about a million times before I got in so I called her back. She was calling you but she asked me to come along."

Steve lay down on his own bed. "Forget it. Trolleys don't run to her ritzy dump. Or busses. And I'm too old to hitch."

"She's sending a car." Rube was slyly triumphant. "Haig Armour's car."

Steve frowned. He didn't get it unless two and two were actually four and she was one of Haig's little helpers.

Rube continued. "She said Haig said he'd be delighted to pick us up. He's invited too."

He would be. Haig and his damn car and damn driver. "How the hell did she find me?"

"She said it was easy. She just started calling Hollywood hotels until she found this one."

"You go," Steve decided. "Say you couldn't find me."

"I couldn't do that. It was you she wanted."

It wouldn't hurt to go; wouldn't hurt to find out for sure what Haig Armour expected to get out of him. He yawned, "Okay, you win. But you take on whats-her-name."

"Feather," Rube admitted sadly.

"My God." He climbed off the bed. "I'll take on the cocktails. What about your pals? Find them?"

Reuben was embarrassed. "I found where they used to be. They've already shipped out." He went on quickly. "I'm getting out of here, don't worry about that, Steve. Only I'd sort of like to take in that cocktail party first."

Steve laughed, "I'm not trying to get rid of you." Maybe there'd been pals, maybe not; maybe Reuben St. Clair was a dog on his heels. It was better to have him underfoot than to have to spy out a stranger. If he was just a soldier with no place to go, he'd come in handy to keep Schmidt's boys out of the room. "You might as well stay on with me as long as you're parked here. We don't seem to get in each other's way."

"You mean it?" The boy was appealingly grateful. "It's a lot better kicks than being alone. I don't like to make out alone. I wouldn't want you to think I'm sponging. I was kind of rocky last night but I cashed a check today." He darted to

35

the jangling phone, said happily, "I sure thank you," and into the phone, "Yeah, we'll be right down."

It was Wilton again. In lobby light he looked like any human being. Not much different from Steve, same build, about the same height, same average face. Same dead pan. He stated, "The car's around the corner," and let them follow him. Haig wasn't in it; Haig had gone on ahead to set the stage.

He put them in the back seat, took his place at the wheel. He drove out Selma, there were lights upstairs and down behind the lace curtains of Mr. Oriole's. It would be worth a penny to see Oriole's face if he beheld Steve Wintress in a Fed car.

Early dusk covered the Strip. Reuben wasn't talkative; he was sight-seeing out the window, getting his kicks out of the scrawled signature of Ciro's, the awning of the Mocambo. Peering into passing Cad convertibles for movie stars. The car followed the old bridle path on Sunset into Beverly. They didn't hesitate at the hotel, yeah, Haig had gone ahead. They rolled up the Canyon and through open gates tonight to the front steps of French Provincial grandeur. The grandeur was sustained. Feather wasn't at the door; a white-coated Philippine boy, twin to the Balboa's elevator operator, took their hats and whispered, "This way, please."

The hall wasn't so much, it only smelled of money with its icy candelabra and polished rosewood. The library, to which they were escorted, was something else. A vasty warm room of books in maple, of soft-patterned couches and deep chairs, of winter roses in silver bowls; a room of giant eucalyptus logs burning in a mammoth white brick fireplace. Haig Armour stood by the fire at the far end of the room, Feather jumped up out of the pillows on the elongated primrose couch. She was dwarfed by the enormity of the room and she looked childlike in the white satin shirt, the slender trousers of blue-black velvet. She'd discarded her horn-rims, her face lifted like a crystal flower out of the satin ruff at her throat.

"I'm so happy you could come," she recited, her pale hair swinging against her cheeks. She didn't say it happy.

Haig was as easy as she was rehearsed. "Hello, Steve. Hello, Reuben. You boys get rested up today?"

Steve said, "Hello," and turned his eyes on the low table with setups of the finest silver and glass.

36

Feather said, "Won't you help yourself? I'm not good at mixing."

Steve poured a good one of bourbon, the best bourbon. He added enough soda, gave place to Reuben, and made himself comfortable on the couch. Reuben and Haig carried their drinks over to the bookshelves as if they were interested in literature. His eyes followed them briefly, returned to the girl. He punched a cushion, his fist sinking into the down and leaving no imprint. "Sit down, lady," he directed her. As if he didn't know, he said, "And what do you do for a living?"

She curled in the corner. "Nothing yet. I want to be a dancer."

"Why not?"

"I mean a really good one. It takes so long, and then you're too old."

He tested the drink. Potent. "I used to know a dancer. She was a good one, too. In great demand, every night." You weren't permitted to mix business and liquor. It wasn't orthodox. He got away with it because he could do a dangerous piece of work better than anyone in the outfit. And unless he could do it his way, it wasn't done. They were afraid a guy would start talking if he drank, and on that, they were right. But it wasn't necessary to talk. He never talked unless it came in handy.

Reuben and Haig were still among the books. Steve moved a little closer to Feather, she in turn pushed herself further into the corner cushion. "What do you want to dance for? With this setup?"

"It isn't mine," she said defensively. "My aunt married it." Her fingers were white and rigid against the cushion, as if she would spring if he edged nearer. He wanted to try it just to see how far she could jump. Her question halted him. "Where did she dance?"

"In Berlin." He looked unseeing into the amber of his glass. His voice was hard. "You didn't ask me what she danced for. I'll tell you. She danced for nylons and a good lipstick—and a bed."

Feather sucked in her breath. He turned his head slowly, looked her over from the smooth crown of her petal head, down her thin body to her velvet toes. "You wouldn't, would you? You'd go without. But when you got hungry enough—"

She jumped then. Not because he had moved but because she had an excuse. "Elsabeth," she shrilled. "Come meet my friends." She almost ran the long length of the room to greet this Elsabeth, a slender woman with exquisite golden hair, an exquisite French-cut dress, discreet jewels, and a face that showed her years.

Haig and Reuben returned to the party. Feather said, "This is my aunt, Elsabeth Moritz." She made the introduction before tucking herself again into the couch corner. Steve was surprised that she returned to it.

Elsabeth was polite to Steve and Reuben. But she put herself beside Haig Armour, asked him for a drink. "What a day! I thought the committee would never come to a decision." She didn't identify the committee. She took the tall glass from Haig, the properly made drink, only half filled. "Thanks, so much." Her voice was nicely modulated, her smile had a friendly warmth, yet somehow both were artificial. If you washed away the top layer, you'd find something else; ten to one a hard-boiled kid in the line, bitching her way up the ladder to position and money. From Prospect Park to Benedict Canyon in twelve tough steps. Steve rather liked her.

"Eldon not here yet?" she asked Feather. "Poor dear. The shooting schedule on this new epic is simply gruesome. You know how Danton is." She was confidential about Danton in the rueful lift of eyebrows.

Haig said, "I'm a great admirer of your husband's work, Mrs. Moritz. I've wanted to meet him for a long time."

She accepted the compliment with a gracious inclination of her head. Haig carried on, mentioning details of one picture and another. Either he was an honest fan or he'd done a lot of research today. Steve didn't think Haig had that much time for movie-going.

Steve said to Feather, "Last movie I saw was Casablanca. It was good too."

She waited to see if it were a joke. When he didn't laugh, she asked, "Really?"

"Sure."

She'd evidently been briefed to take care of him because she kept her cat eyes on his face, just as if he were revealing something important. If she were expected to make friends with him, he'd make it easy for her. He'd get more from this awkward kid than from Haig Armour. The man's polish was the real stuff but it didn't affect the steel beneath.

"How about you and me and Rube having a bit of dinner later on?"

38

For a moment she didn't answer. Then she breathed, "I'm sorry. Haig's already asked me."

He wasn't surprised. "He's too old for you, baby. And I'd say Rube's a bit too young." He winked at her, let her think the bourbon was responsible. "Now I'm just about right." He reached out his hand to pat her velvet knee and watched her shrink back into the corner. He didn't know whether it was he who scared her or any man with ideas. "How about it?"

She said, "I can't." She wasn't sorry. "I've already accepted his invitation."

"In that case," Steve announced, "I'll have another drink." He went first to Reuben's chair. The soldier was odd man; he was sitting there quietly as if he were at home in the rich room. Steve put his hand on the khaki shoulder. "How you doing, fella?"

The grin was ready. "Looks kind of like you're taking on the drinks and the girl both."

Steve nodded portentously. "Just softening her up for you, kid." He was at the setups when Eldon Moritz appeared at the far archway.

Elsabeth lifted her voice, you had to lift your voice for it to carry that far. "You're frightfully late, dear. You'll have time for just one drink before we dress."

He said, "Oh God, what tonight?" He approached with quick, nervous steps.

"Come meet Feather's friends. Dinner with Marty before we go to the *première* of his latest."

Moritz was a neat man, almost dapper in his pin-striped suit and discreetly handsome Charvet cravat. He had no resemblance to an artist, rather he was the tired business-man, his dark hair receding to baldness on his long head, his mustache two pencil strokes, dark crayon under his eyes.

His wife introduced Haig and didn't remember the other names. Steve presented himself and gestured, "Reuben St. Clair." Eldon mixed himself a double rye as he acknowledged the introductions. He drank before asking Reuben, "Any relation to Stryker St. Clair?"

Rube wriggled. "My father, sir."

"Thought so. Family resemblance. We were at Princeton together." He joined his wife and Haig.

Steve re-estimated the kid fast. Not Sinclair, St. Clair; his old lady and new boy friend would be stashed up on Park Avenue, not in some cold-water flat; Stryker St. Clair was a Dun and Bradstreet name, an old Blue Book name, a new

39

café society name. It hadn't been orders to stick with Steve. Just a poor rich boy, a lonesome kid, looking for a friend, not a free ride. You could get too suspicious.

Steve swerved back to Feather. "Want to change your mind about tonight, baby?"

She'd been looking long at Haig but she jumped her attention to Steve as he spoke. She tried to turn on a little charm but she wasn't much good at it. "Why not tomorrow night?"

"I may not be around tomorrow night."

Her pale eyes studied him, looking for the joker in this. He expanded, "I'm on a quick job."

Her lashes flickered. It could have been admiration; it could have been relief that he wouldn't be bothering her any longer. Reuben was taking it easy, maybe dreaming he was back home with the folks. Haig and Eldon were being technical about movies, Elsabeth was timing them. Steve leaned to Feather. He was confidential. "You ought to latch onto Rube while you've got a chance. Get yourself a dump like Auntie, swimming pools and all the fixings. You heard who your uncle said he was."

She was softly indignant. "What makes you think I want these things? Do you consider it fair that Eldon Moritz can spend a hundred thousand dollars on this house while whole families are living in one room?"

"He works for it, doesn't he?"

"It isn't Eldon," she returned quickly. "He has a conscience. It's just the whole capitalist system where such things can happen." She bit her lip as if she'd spoken out of turn.

Steve didn't swallow bait. He undertoned, "I think I'll have another capitalistic bourbon while it's free to the peasants. How about you?"

"I don't drink." She was prim.

"Then you aren't a hundred-per-cent, red-blooded peasant. We take when the taking's good from these rich bastards."

No one saw how weak he poured it. Elsabeth was demanding, "We must run, Eldon. Marty won't forgive us if we make him late for his own *première*." Eldon didn't like leaving when the party was centered about his abilities, but he finished his glass. Elsabeth performed a gracious goodby all around, Eldon nodded distractedly to the unknowns and suggested to Haig, "Let's have lunch. I want to explain my message in that one." He followed his wife.

40

Feather smiled timidly at Haig. "I'd better change too." She skipped after the others, to report to them too?

Steve waited only until she was out of sight. "I don't get her. What's she scared of?"

"You." Haig had an amused eyebrow.

"Me?"

"She was quiet as a pond until you arrived." He was again at the bookshelves. "A real artist, Moritz." He pulled a book, riffled through it. "Did you read about the excitement at the airport last night?"

Reuben asked, "You mean the guy found dead of a heart attack?"

Heart attack, hell. Haig Armour knew better; he wouldn't be mentioning it if he didn't know more than what the news vendors were putting out.

"If either of you had wandered outside when you were looking for your friends, you'd have discovered him."

"Yeah." Steve elongated the word as in admiration of Armour's imagination. "Too bad we didn't." Despite precautions, had the law someway tied Steve up with Albion? Or was Haig fishing? Because Steve Wintress's name and its implications weren't unknown to him?

Haig replaced the book. It made a slight click returning to the shelf. Like a gun cocking. "The man was waiting for our plane." He said it pleasantly. But he was watching Steve.

Steve handed him one. "Was he waiting for you?"

Haig shook his head.

"Then how do you know about it?" He couldn't play it innocent like Rube, he wasn't the type. He had to settle for the wise-guy attitude of the half drunk.

"One of the attendants at the airport remembered his questions regarding our flight." Haig was extraordinarily careful with his cigarette ash. It made a soft gray capsule in a translucent jade tray. "The odd thing is that no one from the flight turned up to identify him."

This time Steve didn't hesitate. "You must have had a special interest in this guy the way you've been looking into him."

Haig didn't have to respond. Feather's appearance in the arch was sufficient diversion. She'd changed to a slender black dress and pulled up her hair in an effort for sophistication. It didn't amount to enough.

But Haig chose to answer. "I'm always interested in oddi-

41

ties." He dropped the subject there. "Why don't you fellows come along to dinner with us?"

"Now, we wouldn't want to move in," Reuben began.

"Why not?" Steve decided. The way a guy with too many quick ones could be expected to perform. "Why not? Why let Mr. Armour have all the fun?" He gulped the rest of his drink.

Haig asked, "You don't mind, Feather?"

She said, "Oh no," but she wasn't quite sure. She did it pretty well. Just as if she and Haig hadn't planned the whole layout before Wilton delivered Steve and Reuben into their hands. As to what they wanted, Steve still wasn't too sure.

2

As host, Haig Armour took over even as he had the night before. There was no choice of café; the party arrived at Haig's hotel. He swept them to a reserved table in the glossy dining room, allowed them to inspect the mammoth menu and exquisite wine list while he ordered. No one opposed. You didn't oppose a torrent.

He timed his grenade until they were lulled by luxury.

"I understand you boys are from Berlin." He didn't bother to explain where he'd picked up the information. "Did you happen to run across a fellow there called Davidian?"

No one stopped eating.

Reuben shook his head. "Uh-uh." He dug into his oyster cocktail.

Steve made a play at trying to place the name. "Davidian? Don't think I did. What's his racket?"

Haig smiled. "You might say he's an artist."

You might say that. An engraver could be called an artist, that is, if he were as artistic an engraver as Davidian. He could make money you'd have a hard time telling from the real thing. The Germans had known it; that explained why he didn't end up a handful of bones or ash. The Russians had found out about him; they'd cleared him with dispatch of any Nazi stain. The Americans had a file on his talents. And another one on his activities.

"Friend of yours?"

"No," Haig answered with the same offhand smile. "But a friend of mine went to Berlin to meet him."

Steve asked, "Was he worth it?"

"He wasn't there. He'd disappeared."

Somehow the word, simple enough in itself, assumed a

sinister quality, something foreign to the elegance of dinner in Beverly Hills. Feather's hands were nervous at the celery dish. Reuben put away his oyster fork. It was he who asked, "Disappeared?"

Haig studied the boy briefly. He nodded.

Steve wondered. Could it be Haig didn't know which one of the two was looking for Davidian?

"From the American zone?" Rube probed.

"From the Eastern sector."

Steve narrowed his eyes on Haig. "How did your friend expect to find him if he was in the Russian sector? The Reds don't like Americans poking around in their business."

Reuben said, "That's a fact," and launched a couple of anecdotes about guys he'd known who had tried to wander over the boundary. He even brought up the old familiar friend of a friend who had vanished on a harmless foray. Haig listened courteously.

The girl turned her head to Steve with pallid indignation. "We wouldn't want them poking into our business either." It was evident that she'd been primed to get him popping off. Her earlier guff about capitalism was part of the same. He let Reuben answer her.

"But their guys don't disappear over on our side. We just bounce them back fast."

Haig lit a cigarette. "I'm trying to find Davidian." Was he angling for an informer? Did he hope that Steve would sell out to him; could it be he had heard that Steve worked for hire, not devotion to a cause? The waiters were a stylish drill team, removing plates, making order out of disorder before bringing the steaks.

Steve hooted. "In Beverly Hills?"

Haig lifted bold eyes. "Does that surprise you?" He knew it didn't. He might think Rube was playing a hand in this, but he knew Steve Wintress was in Los Angeles for only one purpose.

Steve asked innocently, "Why would a man like that turn up here?"

Haig shrugged. "Possibly to meet a very good friend of his. Janni Zerbec."

Somehow the glass in Steve's hand didn't splinter. All of them were eying him. If he didn't brazen it out, Haig would wonder out loud what was bothering him. He brazened, "Is Janni Zerbec here?"

"Yes, Tim saw her today." Haig was casual. "You know her?"

Janni wasn't one for idle talk, certainly not to the Gestapo. Yet she didn't know the shape of U.S. officialdom. It wasn't the ugly iron spikes or hunks of jagged stone she was conditioned to; it was clerks like Timothy or smooth operators like Haig Armour. She wouldn't know how dangerous they could be. Steve decided to play it dumb. If she'd mentioned his visit to Timothy, he would brand her a liar. Let Haig prove which one lied.

"Isn't she the girl who used to dance in those black-market cafés?" If only Feather couldn't add. If only she'd forgotten the earlier moment of his indulgence in remembering Janni. His question sounded genuinely curious; this Berlin pin-up of earlier G. I.'s shouldn't be linked with his personal bitterness over a dancer. He grimaced. "The joints out of bounds for us G. I.'s?"

Feather's wide eyes widened. "You mean she danced for G. I.'s and lived in the Eastern sector?"

"Maybe she couldn't read the signs," Rube said dryly.

Haig's eyes hadn't moved from Steve. "You were in Berlin with the Army of Occupation?"

"I was one of the first guys in."

Reuben's smile wrapped Steve up in a new blanket of friendship. The kid would have been in high school when Steve was rolling into Berlin. The old men had been sent home, the high school crowd had taken over. Same job, no modern improvements. There wasn't even a concept of peace any longer between wars. Nothing but stalemate between Armageddons.

Steve became garrulous in imitation of old soldiers. "There were plenty of girls entertaining us conquering heroes. But only one Janni Zerbec. Everybody knew Janni."

"Off bounds," Haig commented.

Something in the way he said it made Steve ask what he didn't want to ask. "Did you?"

Haig had been waiting for this. He let his smile grow reminiscent, his dark eyes slumberous. "Yes, I knew her."

Steve managed to speak evenly. "You were over there, too, when the war ended?"

"I was there ahead of the lines."

And Haig could have lined her up before Steve found her. It wasn't true. Steve was sure it wasn't true. This lie was a part of Haig's master plan, only that; something labeled Operation Davidian, with Directive A: dissect Steve Wintress; Subdirective: try Stimulus Janni. And watch Steve Wintress bleed. It wasn't going to work. Haig couldn't hear
44

his heart thudding: *Keep your fine manicured paws off Janni, keep your richness for the Feathers—keep away from Janni!* Haig could hear only the question he spoke aloud, "What the hell's she doing here?"

Haig said, "Perhaps Davidian will answer that."

Davidian shouldn't have made contact with her; he'd been warned to stay away from anyone out of his past. Steve asked bluntly, "Are you out here to ship them back to Berlin?"

Haig laughed, "They appear to be here legitimately." He stopped laughing. "Unless they move into the wrong crowd." The waiters were again tidying up the table. "Besides it's not my business. I'm in a different racket now, as you would put it. My doctor advised a quieter job."

Like hell. Somehow Steve managed a smile. "So you're looking for Davidian to ask him about his income tax."

Rube told the waiter, "I'll have chocolate layer cake with my ice cream."

"In a way." Haig continued smoothly, "You might say I'm interested in the amount of money he's made this year."

Did Haig honestly believe that Davidian was opening up his engraving business in Los Angeles? It was the kind of maneuvering the department had found successful before; it might be tough to apprehend a guy for murder or wife-beating or subversive activities, but you could move in fast on income tax irregularities. You could use the threat to bargain for the report.

Haig was asking, "Do you get out here often?"

"No." They couldn't pin on him the coincidence of Davidian and Janni being in these parts.

"I find it a particularly interesting community. It has a heterology of its own but it isn't easy to be lost in it as it is in New York, for example, or Berlin or London. For a fairly simple reason. It doesn't have the ancient warrens of those tired old cities. It is difficult to find a hiding place in a meadow or on the plains. Or in the wide sprawling spaces of Los Angeles. There's too much daylight and not enough shadow."

Steve said sardonically, "Then you won't have much trouble in running down this Davidian."

"Not much." Haig was complacent. "This community has another aspect which is both peculiar and helpful. It is neighborly. Unlike New York, or Berlin or London, where there is, you might say, a psychotic revulsion against so much as recognizing a stranger, the good people here open

45

their arms in welcome. Therefore, undue reticence creates conversation; it actually becomes suspect. And conversation ripples like a pebble in a pond, to the milkman and the breadman and the ice cream man, in the supermarket and the laundromat and the P. T. A. meeting. Whenever I see street after street of neat little white houses, or pink or green or yellow houses, I know that even the children playing on the walks will recognize the presence of a deviationist."

He had it all tagged so neatly. Yet Davidian had hidden out for months now. Successfully. Perhaps Davidian himself had perceived the pattern, perhaps he was hiding in the open. The danger in this solution was obvious; the kids on the block would be singing about the nice new man instead of the nasty new man. You couldn't win the way Haig had outlined it. And Haig could be right; he wouldn't often be wrong.

An urgency to get back to Janni rode Steve's nerves. She'd have to tell him where Davidian was; the F.B.I. had come too far. It wasn't safe for any of them now.

3

It wasn't easy to get away. He didn't doubt this had been one of the purposes of Haig's fancy dinner. To keep him from his job. He made his exit on a palpable excuse about business, insurance business, leaving the three of them at the table, still tied up with coffee and dessert and the check. He caught a cab discharging a couple outside the hotel, announced, "The Biltmore," loudly, in case Haig had a man hanging around. There was no cab waiting to follow and no car took out after him. It was a long ride, not as long as by trolley and bus, and not as time-consuming. But the expense account wouldn't stand many of these jaunts. He'd have to get hold of a car if he was going to track down Davidian in these wide open spaces. Moreover, a cab was too easy to follow.

He played the game in the Biltmore Hotel. The lobby was full of conversation, businessmen in responsible business suits. He couldn't spot a tracker. He went to the desk, asked for a guy who had vanished into Siberia a year back, not a name Haig could check quickly. From there he went to the house phone, put through a call to 819. No one was in earshot when he made it brief to the wrong number at the other end. A fancy flight of steps led to the elevator. He took them fast, caught an elevator waiting, before his call could be traced. He rode to five, a middle-aged couple got off ahead of him but they minded their own business, heading to a room, opening the door and closing it after them. After that he wasted no time in the rug-hushed corridor. He was quick to the fire stairs and he descended on foot. He left by the side door of the hotel.

There weren't too many people walking around the downtown streets at this hour until he reached Main. Its garish honky-tonks were going full blast. He sauntered along, despite the urgency pressing him. Plenty of movie houses cut their marquee lights and let the cashiers go home before midnight. By sauntering he didn't make noticeable his examination of the girls remaining on duty.

She hadn't been lying about her job. She was in the glass cage at one of the meanest of the dumps, leaning on her elbow looking at nothing. When she saw him, the half-smile was turned off. "What do you want?"

"I want to talk to you."

"I have nothing to say to you." She made sure he'd know she meant it by glancing over her shoulder for the bouncer. It was the first time Steve had taken notice of the man by the entrance door, a tall, thin punk with sideburns and greasy black curls. Probably considered himself baby's little protector because she let him walk home with her on nights when she hadn't anything better to do.

"I think you have. I've been with the F.B.I. tonight."

She doubted it.

"They were talking about you."

She asked harshly, "Why can't you leave me alone?" The punk was watchful, ready to step across the miniature lobby and make something of Steve.

"You know why."

She said, "I can't talk on the job."

"What time are you off?"

"Not until two."

"I'll be waiting."

Slim was advancing, one foot at a time, as if he found nothing very interesting in bouncing gents with ideas. Steve shambled off. He didn't want to hit the punk. It wasn't the poor guy's fault.

There were plenty of saloons on the street but he needed a place where he could keep an eye on her, a place where she'd know he was watching and that she couldn't pull a sneak. A decent little Italian restaurant was further up the street on the opposite pavement. It didn't have to hide its

47

business behind curtains. Steve bought the morning paper at the corner and gave it a try. There weren't half a dozen people inside including the help. He took the front corner table; it didn't give him much of a view of her cage but it would do. He didn't want coffee and crullers but they would permit him to hang around. He'd have a long wait; it wasn't yet midnight.

Steve glimpsed the headlines in the paper, the four horsemen galloping there as usual, and as he glanced across the way again he almost upset his coffee. She was leaving the cage, the fellow was going to take her place. He waited to see which way she moved, watched her shrug a coat about her shoulders, watched the punk hand her her purse, his hand lingering stickily on hers.

When she cut across towards the restaurant, Steve relaxed. She wasn't trying to run out. He picked up his paper, kept at it even when she came into the place. He heard her speak, "Just coffee, Pepe." He didn't hear what else she said, she might have been asking Pepe to throw the bum out. Steve kept reading the paper. Until she came to the table, carrying her coffee cup. Until she sat down with him.

He didn't get out of his chair. It wasn't the custom on Main Street. He said, "You're off early tonight."

"I'll make it up tomorrow night." She gulped at the coffee just as if it were good, set the cup down and began fishing in her handbag. "Not that it matters to you."

"Have one of mine?" Steve handed over his cigarette pack.

"So you are paying for information now?"

He didn't answer, he lit her cigarette. She loosed her red coat, it was bargain basement but it was red, and she wore it with a flair. Her dress was a cheap shiny satin, too shiny. On her it had more style than Feather Talle would have dressed by Adrian.

"What story did you give that bum?"

"He is no bum. He is the assistant manager. I explained to him that you were my cousin and that you became ugly when you drank too much. I would have to get you home or there would be trouble."

"And he believed it."

"He could observe you had been drinking." She swallowed more of her coffee. "As could I."

"Not that much." He pushed his crullers to her, she'd eat anything. "Did you tell Davidian that I was looking for him?"

"I do not know where Davidian is."

48

He caught her wrist in pincer fingers. As if she were handling poisoned barbs, she removed them one by one. "You will not touch me."

"Sorry." He wasn't. He was in a churn of anger. "But you can stop lying. I'm not the only one who knows better."

"I do not lie."

He tried again. "You know how to get in touch with him."

"No." He was ready to slam her when she added through an airy swirl of smoke, "He knows how to get in touch with me."

He hopped on it too eagerly. "You've seen him."

"No."

"Janni!" She must realize that time couldn't wait on her tricks. "When will you see him?"

"When he so chooses."

Had they been alone, he might have rattled the truth out of her scornful mouth. They weren't alone. They were in a restaurant where she was Pepe's friend and Steve was her drunken cousin. Because she was pleased at infuriating him, he tried patience. "If you had to get to him in a hurry—"

"There is no way."

She lied. She was too clever to let Davidian escape her. She was as experienced as he, more experienced, in the sly twists of the underground. What Steve didn't get was why Davidian had delivered himself into her hands in the first place. The first contact could have been accidental, but why continue it? Davidian knew her record. It wasn't much different from his own; two guttersnipes out for what they could get. They'd never trusted each other, their only link had been Steve. And then all at once he did know. Davidian needed an address. Someone to pass on his pay to him.

He said, "The F.B.I. is after him."

She was unmoved. "For what reason? He does not work."

"One of their men came to see you today."

Pellets of rage flecked her words. "You set that goat on me!"

"Don't be a fool," he advised sharply. "The last thing I wanted was for them to know about you. Haig Armour sent him."

She spoke unfamiliar syllables. "Haig Armour." Her English wasn't proficient enough to take it other than phonetically. "Who is this?"

"One of your Berlin playmates." Anger was coming up

49

into his throat again. "You couldn't forget Haig Armour. He is rich, important, a magnificent man."

"No, I could not forget this kind! It is because I have this rich, magnificent protector that I live in a hovel with the old ones and work at nights on lower Main Street." She thought about it. "I did not know him."

"He knew you were here," he pointed out. "He sent Timothy Leonard to talk to you. What did Leonard want to know?"

"Where is Davidian? What else would he want? To carry me to his rich—"

He cut in. "Did he mention me?"

"Perhaps he just mentions your name. I do not know this Steve Wintress, Stefan." Her eyes slitted. "What do you tell this man of me?"

"Nothing."

"Now it is you who are lying."

"Him, nothing. Haig Armour—"

Her temper was rising and his slow smile helped it. "What do you tell him?"

"Nothing he doesn't know. I've heard the name Janni Zerbec. Who hasn't? The babe of Berlin." His hand was above her wrist but he remembered not to touch her. "The dancer in all the best cafés."

She spat. "It was jealousy. I was superior to the café dancers. They were old and spavined. They were afraid to have me be seen. It was for this reason I must dance on the street and in private quarters—"

He asked, "Did you know Reuben St. Clair?"

"Who is this?"

"A G. I. He was in Berlin."

She said, "I do not remember. There were so many soldiers. German soldiers, American soldiers, English, French, Russian soldiers. I do not remember their faces or their names, only what they give to me."

"You've stopped lying," he said insolently. "What about Haig Armour?"

She glowered under her ragged dark bangs. "I have told you I do not know this Haig Armour." Again she gave the name phonetic quality. And he didn't know which one spoke true, she or Haig. She was peering past the window. "We have quarreled sufficiently. Now I take you home. You will behave as if I take you against your wishes."

"Who'll believe that?" She couldn't meet his eyes. She hadn't forgotten, no matter how much she wanted to, no matter how much she wanted him to believe she had. He put on a scowl as she walked him out of the place. The fellow who'd taken over her job could watch them depart.

They turned west at Third Street. She said, "Here you may leave me."

He countered, "I haven't the faintest intention of leaving you. I am here for information."

She flashed, "There is no information I can give you. Or your friends. Tell them that. Tell them to leave me alone. I know nothing. Nothing!"

"You know one thing, Janni. How to put me in touch with Davidian. Listen to me." He took her arm, holding it rigid until she ceased resisting. "He is expecting me. We planned this before he left Berlin. It is essential I see him before the others do." They walked together. "Just why are you holding out on me? Hasn't he told you he wants to see me?"

She said savagely, "Maybe he trusts you. I know better."

"What's your percentage?" He flung the insult. "You think you can make a better deal?"

She was trembling with anger. "I would not touch your deals. I wish only to be a good American." The anger subsided. "This is what he wishes also, only to be a good American."

He ignored the appeal. "Davidian looks out for Davidian."

"You do not know him now! He is no longer a man to be beaten, kicked—he is free! I will not turn him over to you to be trapped again in your dirty organization."

"Listen," he demanded. "This hasn't anything to do with any organization. This is a private matter between Davidian and me." He stressed it. "No one else figures in it."

"You are working for the party."

"I work where I get paid." How much did he dare say? It wasn't safe to deposit information with anyone. Not on this kind of job. He couldn't trust her.

Her voice was a smooth, cold stone. "I do not understand this. That you can work for them, betray your own people. For money!"

"It's a good enough reason," he said callously. "You're the last one to point the finger. Let's leave my conscience out of it. And yours. All I want is for you to get word to Davidian that I'm here looking for him. That's all. Not next week or the day after tomorrow. Now. Let him decide if he'll see me. You can believe it or not but if I don't get to him fast, he's in for trouble."

51

"Where you are, there is always trouble," she stated.

He hadn't realized it but they were at the Fifth Street incline that led to Bunker Hill. Without warning she twisted her arm from his clutch. "Stay away from me. I have enough troubles." She began to run up the hill.

He could have followed her. But he didn't. He'd given her enough to think about. She might not recognize it as truth but he had told her true; he had to see Davidian alone before either side moved in.

4

On the long trolley run back to the hotel, he had time to think about Davidian. No matter how much Janni wanted to believe that Davidian had changed, Steve knew better. He was using Janni.

The man could be yet hiding out in the battered old house where Janni lived. This Steve doubted. It would not have been safe for either of them. Wherever Davidian was, it must be a place where there was sufficient seclusion for him to work on his report. It would be a poor place, the old man's purse strings wouldn't pry any wider than small change. But not too isolated, Davidian wasn't the recluse type; he'd be needing someone to smoke a cigarette with, to argue philosophy and politics and historical accidents with. He'd be needing a woman. Wherever he was, he'd make friends. Not caring that friends could be dangerous. For Davidian, danger was the norm.

There was some pattern of communication worked out between the two. They wouldn't risk letters. They would be wary of the telephone. Their good Americanization program would not as yet have erased the deep-rooted suspicion carried with them from Europe. They could meet accidentally, two strangers on a park bench, exchanging the hour; two strangers passing on the street. The solution was so obvious—the all-night movie. Where Janni could be found every night; where Davidian was only another shabby man buying a seat to rest his skinny bones. He could have been inside the grimy theater tonight while she led Steve away by his nose. He cursed her just above his breath. God-damn little slut.

If he'd been in a position to offer her a wad of dollars, she'd have sold him a ticket and personally ushered him to a seat beside the man he sought. Haig had the wad; all he needed was to offer her enough to overcome her repugnance at selling out to the police. Once he caught on to that, events would move fast enough Haig's way. The worst of it was that Steve didn't dare ask for extraordinary funds from the organization; he had to work cheap. While time closed in inexorably.

The trolley trundled past the hotel and Steve jammed the bell. He swung off at the next stop, annoyed at overriding his destination; it meant he was off key and he couldn't afford that. It hadn't to do with the physical actuality of Janni; he was through with that. He could touch her wrist, her arm, without his blood remembering.

He walked back the two blocks. The lobby smoldered in its customary shadow, the nonexistent clerk posed behind the desk, the Philippine boy rode him silently to the fourth floor. He opened the door with his key, saw Reuben leaning against the bath door and then saw the upheaval of the room.

"What the hell?"

"Don't jump me. I just got in."

There'd been so little to disturb, he and Rube traveled light. But that little was upside down on the dirty rug. They hadn't taken his gun; it was a dull high light on the rug. Rube couldn't help spotting it but he didn't say a word.

"The lousy bastards." It wasn't his side, they would have searched the place unobtrusively twelve hours ago. Leaving no traces. Nor would the F.B.I. leave a mess. Not unless they chose to. This was Haig Armour's idea, more psychological unnerving. Steve tossed the gun into his valise. "Sorry." He began to pick up the rest of the stuff.

"You're up to your neck in something, aren't you?"

Steve shook his head. "Just a job. Run of the mill."

"It's tied up with Haig Armour."

"Believe me, kid, I never saw him before last night. Purely accidental."

"He said you'd gone to meet a girl."

"Wise guy." Stripped, he lay on the bed, finishing his nightcap cigarette.

"She got more on the ball than Feather?"

"Wouldn't take much for that."

"Feather's a funny girl. She acts scared." Rube cut the lamp but the neon glow from the cocktail bar across the street gave low-key visibility. He'd forgotten to pull the lank curtains across the windows. It was just as well, maybe the sun would wake them. If there was sun in the morning.

"Scared of men. Except for Uncle Haig. The protective

53

type." Steve wondered out loud, "What did you do after I left?"

"We danced. But she had to get home early. She had a lesson or something in the morning, she said."

"Who took her home?"

"Well, I did. In Haig's car."

"And Haig's chauffeur." Steve added, "Who subsequently delivered you here."

"Right. He doesn't act much like a chauffeur." Rube creaked to an elbow. "Haig's kind of a curious guy."

"About what?"

"You and me. Shacking up here. He kept trying to make out we'd known each other in Berlin. And this girl you two had been talking about."

Steve asked it. "You didn't run into this Janni Zerbec over there?"

"If I did, she didn't tell me her right name. The ones I met were all named Greta."

Steve wasn't going to be a curious guy. Any more than Rube was, not one word about the gun. He'd just go on wondering where Reuben fit or if he fit. At least he had the kid at hand, or vice versa as the case might be.

The room wasn't much brighter when he woke than when he'd slept. Another fog-bound morning. Winter in California. When he emerged from the shower, Reuben was stirring. "What time?"

Steve pushed his last clean shirt into his belt. "Almost eleven. I've got some business to attend to. Think you can keep out of trouble?"

Rube grinned. "I kind of thought I'd go down to the broadcasting studios today. Maybe I'll win us a washing machine."

Steve knotted his tie. "If you don't we better find us a laundry." He slipped into his jacket, took another look at the sky and grabbed his hat and coat. "See you later." He rode downstairs, picked up the morning papers at the corner newsstand, and made for the nearest lunch room. While he waited for his ham and eggs, he drank coffee and searched for mention of Albion. There wasn't any. Albie had moved out of the news as unassumingly as out of existence. No one was interested in him now but the F.B.I.

Steve left the papers with his tip and continued up the boulevard. The sun was beginning to clear away the overcast, pushing small tatters of blue through the dirty gray. He didn't need his topcoat after all. The giant green tin

54

Christmas trees were picking up a glint, the shiny silver ornaments swinging above were turning to silver.

He was on Mr. Oriole's porch exactly at noon, pushing the bell while the hands on his watch met at the top of the dial. Mr. Oriole didn't open the door; it might have been his wife, might have been his mother. She was heavy-hipped with worn hands and shoulders. Her tongue said brokenly, "Come in." She pointed to the parlor. "In here."

No one was in the parlor. Steve didn't sit down. He looked out the side window at a straggle of pale little flowers against the neighboring fence.

Mr. Oriole had slept in the same clothes. He came in complaining feebly, "You're right on time." A thin sheaf of papers dropped from his pudgy fingers.

"I planned it that way." Steve held out his hand. "You have the information?"

"I have done the best I could. You did not give me much time."

"I don't have much time." Steve kept the hand extended. The sharp bell was a rasp across nerve ends. No wonder the woman had looked tired with that racket interrupting her days and nights.

Oriole said nervously, "That will be Mr. Schmidt."

"A conference." It wasn't unexpected.

Schmidt said only, "Good morning," yet somehow in the two words he conveyed distaste for Oriole's uncouth appearance and his displeasure that Steve was here first.

Steve answered the good morning briefly and turned on Oriole. "I told you I have no time to waste. Let's see what you've turned up." He forestalled Oriole's move to pass the papers to Schmidt by stepping up and taking them. He returned to the window, teetered on the edge of a straight-backed chair, his shoulder to the other men. He covered the sparse accounts rapidly; reread, pausing where there might be a clue, then slapped the sheaf on the edge of the fern table. The fronds trembled. Schmidt had to cross the room to retrieve the document.

"So this is all I get." Steve didn't hide disgust. "Davidian came to L.A. maybe seven or eight months ago and checked in at a Bunker Hill apartment house, boarding with a girl named Janni Zerbec and an old couple who might be her kin. By the time we got on to this, Davidian was gone. Vanished. Being thorough, Albion called at the apartment, a broken-down, one-room affair. He didn't see how they could take in a boarder." Steve grimaced. "Albion must have

55

forgotten his Berlin experience. He found out nothing from the old couple, they don't speak English, only some obscure Slav dialect. The girl spoke English but persisted in knowing nothing. She admitted Davidian had moved out, she had no idea where. Why did he move? Perhaps because he found a better place, perhaps because he no longer had the money to pay board to them. The girl was in no way cooperative in her responses. She insisted Davidian had been gone from there for six months."

Schmidt had retired to the couch. He was following the report by eyeglass as well as by ear. Steve got to his feet and began to pace the mottled carpet as he had yesterday. To focus attention on himself.

"Albion alerted certain trusted workers to check the obvious places. The missions were investigated, the Skid Row charity joints, the county jail. Davidian wouldn't be the first bum to take advantage of bed and board on the town. The investigators were hampered by having no first-hand knowledge of Davidian, no photograph, merely Albion's memory of a man he met maybe once or twice five years ago. The official description's vague enough, about forty years old, sallow complexion, dark eyes and hair, small hands and feet, height five feet four or five. It fits dozens. And easy enough to change that description in six months with good American food and California sun." He broke off sharply. "I wasn't sent here to walk the streets looking for a familiar face under a new disguise. I'm here to pick up the Davidian report. That's my job. To get the Davidian report."

"You knew he had disappeared," Schmidt said.

"Davidian was supposed to be located before I got here. Albion was closer than this or he wouldn't have alerted me to come. He wouldn't waste my time. Where's his report?" His hand was all-encompassing scorn of the papers Schmidt clenched. "Hack work. From hack workers. All of it ending in a big round zero. The girl used to walk through Pershing Square at noon. It could have been to feed the pigeons; it could have been that she was aware of a certain face in the line-up of derelicts loafing on the benches. Who knows? She never spoke to anyone, not while our hacks were around." He said unpleasantly, "So the Square's been chewed up, maybe I should burrow in the debris and see if Davidian's hiding under a hunk of dirt? Albion could have given me Davidian. Albion's dead."

"It is unfortunate."

He hated Schmidt's guts, the righteous son of a bitch. "Yeah, unfortunate."

Schmidt said stiffly, "I was referring to Albion's refusal to conform to the imperative of sharing his total information with our committee. It is unfortunate that he was of a secretive nature. He did not report fully to us."

Steve menaced, "Are you saying he reported to someone else?"

"We do not know," Schmidt said evenly. "We do know he was frequenting the offices of the F.B.I."

"No!" They couldn't believe that. Not even Schmidt could believe that Albion had been ratting to the F.B.I. If Schmidt had had Albion liquidated there was something more behind it, Schmidt's jealousy of a more important worker, or his rage at being unable to force Albion to rigid conformance. Schmidt would find out how unfortunate it was that Albion was gone. After Steve turned in his report to Berlin. "I don't believe it."

"It is authenticated."

A narrow cold man who couldn't see beyond the dogma on his eyeglasses. Or who used that dogma for his own opportunities. Steve said, "There's only one thing that interests me at this moment. Why didn't you get Albion's information before—he died. I'm back where he started weeks ago. With Davidian and a girl."

"You could talk with this girl." Maybe he knew that Steve had seen Janni, maybe not. Schmidt knew too much.

"I've talked with her," Steve admitted. "I got just as far as Albion did. Nothing."

Mr. Schmidt removed his rimless glasses and peered for a dust mote. "There are ways—"

This time Steve could turn the anger loose. "Where do you think you are? Germany? Russia? Or in the funny papers? This is the U. S. You don't go around smashing up women unless you want to pay for it. I don't." He stopped short and pointed a fist at Schmidt. "Just in case you get any more screwball ideas, let me tell you this girl was conditioned under both the Nazis and the occupation. You can liquidate her but you can't squeeze one drop in information out of her. Unless she wants to give it. She wouldn't be alive today if she were intimidatable."

"You know this girl?"

"Yes, I know her." He wasn't certain how much to reveal. Another glance at Schmidt's impassive face and he made the decision; Janni's safety might depend on his putting his personal mark on her. "And maybe I can find out a way to get her to talk, she is the one known link. I'm working on it." He pushed back his hat. "The only trouble is the F.B.I. is hot on her too."

"You had dinner with Haig Armour last night."

Steve made no attempt to reply until he glared through into the colorless eyes. "Yeah," he said softly. And then he shot the question, "Why don't you set your hot-shot spies on finding Davidian instead of checking me? You know," his smile was unpleasant, "I wouldn't be surprised if I turned up the Davidian report despite your help." He swerved to the silent Oriole. "I need a car."

Oriole's eyes faltered to the boss. "This can be arranged?"

"Never mind about arrangements," Steve told him. "I want a car. I'm not a fat capitalist who can hire cabs. If I have to hoof this town, I won't get any further or faster than your stooges."

"You have a car available?" Schmidt asked of Oriole. His distaste of Steve was in his white lips.

"There is my own car. It is not so good—"

"If it runs, it'll do," Steve said.

"This report?" Schmidt questioned. He lifted the papers.

"You know what to do with it." Steve let out a short laugh. "If you get something with a lead in it, let me know."

"Any help we can give you," Schmidt promised dully. "We have assured our friends in New York that we will co-operate with you to the extent of our faculties."

The bastard had checked with New York since the meeting last night. The thorough Mr. Schmidt. New York hadn't phoned him, such preliminaries had been fulfilled through Albion before Steve left for California.

Steve said, "You might try thinking up some answers on Albion's death. For instance, why the F.B.I. should be interested in a heart attack." It would corroborate Albie's treachery in Schmidt's books but it would also let the bastard know that it wasn't as easy to get rid of a man as he might have thought it would be. "They haven't tied him up with me yet but they're worrying it. If they should get too close, I'll want you to divert them."

Schmidt said, "I understand." It was the kind of routine he could carry out. Planning it would keep him busy for another twenty-four hours.

Steve said to Oriole, "Where's your car?"

"It is in my back yard. I will drive it out for you."

"Never mind that." He trod on Oriole's heels. He hadn't expected to get a look at the ground floor layout this early. Behind the portieres was what should have been the back parlor. Obviously Mr. Oriole used it not only for his private office but also as a lunch counter and for naps. A ragged quilt of faded rose and blue was lumped on a scabrous leather couch. The roll-top desk was littered with papers, the stale scraps of a bun, a cup with a scum of yellowed milk over cold dregs, and a plate smeared with what might have been cherry pie. The anachronism was the austerity of green steel filing cabinets. The room smelled unclean, the smell of Oriole. There was a telephone on the desk, a personal line, no coin box.

Mr. Oriole half apologized. "My wife, she has not cleaned in here today, it seems." It was automatic, a little joke he would make whenever anyone viewed his squalid quarters. He divided old-style sliding wooden doors at the right; Steve hadn't seen their like since he was a kid visiting a widowed aunt in upper Manhattan. The dining room was small and drab but neat. In the kitchen the tired woman was scrubbing a wooden sink drain. An electric icebox was the one touch of the twentieth century here.

Steve followed through to the back porch, a clutter of broken relics, a bird cage, a washboard, a child's wicker doll buggy. Mr. Oriole knew the path through the junk; for all his bulk he disturbed not one useless object. Latticework masked the porch from the neighbors. The four splintered steps down into the back yard were unmasked.

The yard was overgrown with weeds and dried grasses. The car stood in the open; it wasn't much, a plain black sedan of too old a vintage. Mr. Oriole took two keys, tied together with soiled twine, from his pocket. He said tenderly, "It runs pretty good. Most the time."

"I'll take good care of it." Steve opened the car door.

Mr. Oriole was pressing over Steve's shoulder. "The lights are here." He pointed a dirty forefinger. "The starter is this one." It wasn't what Mr. Oriole wanted to say. It wasn't why the man's soiled breath was against Steve's neck nor why his back was hunched to hide Steve from anyone looking out the window. Nor was it that Steve might be unable to locate the windshield wiper. The words came fearfully in a whisper, "I could tell you something."

Mr. Oriole pointed to another button but he didn't label it. He was more afraid, having spoken this much.

Steve followed Oriole's lead, pantomiming an examination of the dashboard. He said impatiently, "For Christ sake, go on." He expected it to be about Albion, he went so far as to expect a hint that Schmidt had decreed the same end for Steve Wintress.

"This man came to my house asking for you."

"Which man?"

"The one you call Davidian."

This out of a clear sky. Steve didn't turn on him, he knew the risk Mr. Oriole was taking in confiding the information. "When?"

"It was—" He pondered, his breath heavy. "It was on Monday night."

"Why didn't you—"

"I did not know of you. Mr. Schmidt did not tell me until Wednesday that you were expected. He does not confide in me."

"You knew of Davidian."

"Yes," he admitted. "I did not recognize him. I had not been told of his appearance." He shrugged. "And if I had, there are so many men like him." He tried for a pathetic joke, patting his own big stomach. "He has not become rich and fat in this land of dollars."

He couldn't keep Oriole here too long, Schmidt would become suspicious. Steve slid over in the seat. "Get at the wheel. Start showing me how to start the car, as if it had tricks."

Oriole moved fast for a man of his weight.

"Now give it to me."

"It was early evening. He stood on the porch. I did not invite him in, I did not know him, how could I guess? He asked for you by name. Stefan Winterich. But I had not been told Stefan Winterich was coming to us." He wouldn't soon forget this grievance. "I thought perhaps he had the wrong house number. Or perhaps a trap. We must be so careful always of a police trap."

"Sure," Steve agreed. "Was he on foot or wheels?"

"On foot." Oriole caused the car to give little huffing noises.

"Positive?"

"Of this I am certain." He would have stood peering from behind the lace curtains after the man. "There was no car on the street before he came or after he left. He was a poor man."

This put Davidian in a new location, Hollywood. A far cry from Skid Row. He could have ridden the trolley, the

60

same as Steve. But how had he got on to Mr. Oriole's place unless he'd been sniffing around the Hollywood hangouts?

Mr. Oriole was insistent. "I did not guess, you understand this? How can a man be expected to guess that a stranger . . . I said nothing just now—" His small eyes turned to the house. "I am afraid Mr. Schmidt would not understand this. But he had not told me your name or that you were coming." He was sweating, his shirt smelled.

"Don't tell Schmidt," Steve advised. It was what Oriole wanted to hear. He'd make a mistake and mistakes were not allowed. He'd confessed to it, either because he was afraid he'd be found out or in a sincere effort to be of help. As to whom he should make confession, he'd had to choose between Steve and Schmidt. He'd chosen Steve. He would hope he was backing the right man, he couldn't know. Top men came and went fast in the organization. It would have been a hard decision for Oriole to make; Schmidt was his bread and butter. But Steve might be the marmalade; he was higher up, he must be to have been sent from Berlin to New York to Los Angeles. Unless this whole business was a trap dreamed up by Schmidt and Oriole to put Steve in a spot. You could never be sure of anything.

Steve knew what the answer would be before he asked. "He left no message, nowhere to look for him?"

"Nothing." Mr. Oriole was clambering out of the car. His chins quavered. "You understand why I said nothing?"

Steve said, "As long as you keep on saying nothing you're safe. If Davidian comes back, find out where he lives. If you have to follow him yourself."

"Oh yes. Yes, I will do that."

He slammed the door, stepped on the starter. "If Schmidt wants to know what took you so long, tell him I'm an idiot about machinery."

He backed and filled, got the car into the driveway, and noted the hand holding aside the lace curtains as he rolled past the side parlor window. Mr. Schmidt would not have overlooked the delay. Yet somehow Steve was certain that Mr. Oriole would cover well, that he was long accustomed to protecting his own interests.

III

STEVE DROVE DIRECTLY TO Janni's. Near two o'clock. She should be just about getting up. She'd been in early last night. He knew no short cuts but he knew the direction of town. He had no trouble until he reached the downtown section. It was cut up into a maze, he went in and around tunnels, one-way streets, dead-end streets, long blocks without intersections, before he found the trick of reaching Bunker Hill. He'd have a hard time finding it again. The town was on a building spree; despite government controls, white concrete towers were rising above the scaly old tenements. Steve parked in front of Janni's apartment. He saw no forbidding signs.

The street was as empty of life as it had been previously. He climbed up the old steps to the creaking porch, entered the scabrous hallway and began his longer climb up to her room. There wasn't as much noise through the walls as yesterday, now it was rustles and whispers, but the smell of age and dust and bad cooking was unchanged.

She wouldn't be surprised that he had returned. She knew he didn't give up easily. The old woman's hostile face answered his decisive knock.

He pushed in. "I'm here to see Janni." He didn't care if she understood.

She let loose her unintelligible imprecations. She was probably telling him that Janni wasn't here. She wasn't. Her cot was made up, an old army blanket smoothed over it. The old man sat by the window making fine stitches on a white *glacé* glove. Not enough light sifted in but he didn't need light. After centuries of glove-making, he would sew out of his unconscious. And the dream of a proud and ancient day when he was glove-maker to dukes and queens. He was too old to understand the new order. He didn't raise his dim eyes from his work; an altercation between the

62

old woman and a visitor was too usual, or he was stone-deaf.

Steve demanded, "Where is she?" He pointed to the cot. "Janni?" The old lady started off again but he shouted at her, "You can drop that stuff. You can talk the language enough to tell me."

Out of a sullen mouth she muttered, "She has gone out, fool."

"Where?"

"Her business she does not tell me."

Steve shouted at the old man. "Where did she go?" There was no response. Nothing but cranky fingers and a minute white stitch.

The woman laughed. But she would not speak again.

Steve gave up. "If you find her first, tell her I'm waiting for her." He didn't slam the door behind him out of respect for the ancient craftsman.

He let off steam clattering down the flight of steps, banging out on the porch. And he saw her. She was on the sidewalk coming towards the house, her arms wrapped around a large brown paper sack. She wasn't dressed for company, a yellow scarf imprinted with crimson cabbage roses was tied over her hair; she wore dark slacks and sweater, flat-heeled slippers. She didn't see him until she lifted her eyes before climbing the final flight of steps. He waited there at the top, leaning against the grimy white pillar.

She gave him no greeting. Not until she stood beside him did she speak. "What do you want now?"

"Where have you been?"

"It is perhaps your business?"

She would have walked by him but he stepped in her path. "Did you see Davidian?"

He followed the droop of her eyelids to the green fronds of carrots, the dirt-purple of beets, the dark loaf of bread.

"Oh yes," she said loftily, "I have been driving around in my Cadillac convertible calling upon all my gentlemen friends." She shifted the grocery sack in her arms.

He said, "Let me take it," automatically. She started to pass it into his hands and then with the suddenness of thunder, both were motionless, like children playing statues.

They stood too long, their eyes meeting, before she broke by him. "Go away. I don't want to see you again." She was in the house and the touch of her slippers on the staircase

63

blurred back to his ears before he came alive. He walked on down the steps to the street, got in Mr. Oriole's old car and drove away.

It couldn't be that she had remembered with him, the same moment, the identical, unimportant moment. It had been dusk then and he had been framed in a doorway more shabby than the one on Bunker Hill. Behind him there had been a murky hallway and a staircase as steep and multi-odored as the one she was climbing now. She had come through the blue evening carrying a sack in the same way, her arms wrapped about it in the same way, as if it were a baby she carried. It hadn't been a clean brown paper sack; it was dirty burlap, used over and again. That night she had come laughing and the laughter hadn't left her eyes when she saw him waiting for her. When he said, "Let me take it," she'd passed it over to him, whispering, "Oh, so many good things, Stefan," and she'd followed close on his heels, up, up, up the rotten staircase to the mean little room. . .

His fist clenched until it ached and he beat it on Oriole's steering wheel until pain cut away the ache. He kept his mind on driving then. He watched his speed and the side streets and the confusion of traffic signals. He couldn't afford to be picked up. Not without a driver's license. Not with his reasons for being in the city.

He reached Hollywood Boulevard and slowed further for its traffic. There were new signs from Vine Street north, "Temporary No Parking"; there were service trucks string-ing lights overhead, among the bright tinsel decorations. On either side of the boulevard, men were roping off areas halfway to the trolley lines. Some kind of big doings must be on for tonight.

He made a right turn because it was easier than trying to make it on the left, circled a block and drove past his hotel to a parking lot in the rear. He'd be better off on foot for the next trip. There wasn't going to be any spare parking space on the side streets with the main stem blocked off.

He headed for Highlands; he found the address of Albion's shop easily enough, not more than a half dozen doors around the corner from the boulevard. The layout was just what he'd expected. It was always the same, the Thomas Jefferson or the Thomas Paine bookshop; never any imagination. Never the Benedict Arnold or the Lenin.

This one looked the same as any and all, a small plate-glass front window with books in formula display, popular books of the day in slick jackets, capitalistic books. No lousy

64

propaganda items such as *I Escaped from a Soviet Concentration Camp* or *I Used To Be a Communist Spy*, but no lives of Little Father Stalin either. Good, honest, safe books for the window. Inside you could buy another kind.

Within, the place was neat and small and quiet. There weren't any customers, which could have been the reason the eyes of all three clerks converged on Steve when he entered. He'd seen them all before, in one city after another. A young fellow, tall, dark, intense, horn-rimmed, neat as the shop in his dark suit, his conservative tie; two young women, one blond, one brown-haired; one a little too plump, the other a little too thin; neither pretty, but neither homely; both horn-rimmed, both wearing sweaters and skirts. Both would be hopelessly in love with the young man but he'd have a girl who modeled or did bits on the television screen and who hankered after a director if she couldn't land a producer. She wouldn't give a damn about a brave new world except for herself. And the three would know all these items about each other, whether or not they'd admit such minor matters to be important. They didn't have to worry about frustrations because they had the great bulbous-breasted cause to rest their emotions on.

Steve didn't fool around with any table browsing. He moved back into the store. The young man came towards him. "May I help you?" His voice was almost as good as Haig Armour's, not as flamboyant but with the same upper-class modulations.

"I'm looking for Frederick Grasse."

The girls might have popped side glances at each other, their fingers may have tightened, but the young man was contained. "He isn't here. Is there anything I can do for you?"

"I'll wait." Maybe he could figure a way to get into the office if he hung around. And then he realized he wasn't first with the idea. There was someone coming out of the cubbyhole hidden back there in the gloom.

The three clerks relaxed just a little. You wouldn't know the young fellow needed to relax until he did. He said, "Mr. Grasse won't be in today." And Mr. Schmidt was with them. He hadn't expected Steve.

Steve said, "You're ahead of me." The clerks were surprised that he knew Mr. Schmidt.

"I wished to check personally," Schmidt said.

"Mind if I have a look?"

"Not at all." The reply was too prompt; there'd be noth-

65

ing left for Steve in the cubbyhole. Schmidt pointed his hand at the young man. "Llewellyn, this is Mr. Wintress from New York. A friend of Frederick's."

"Yes, sir." The young man was alert.

"Llewellyn Meadows," Mr. Schmidt identified him. "Assistant manager to Grasse." To the young fellow he said, "You will give Mr. Wintress your co-operation."

"Yes, sir." A well-trained assistant. If Schmidt had said, "You will bump off Frederick Grasse on Wednesday night," would Llewellyn have had no response but, "Yes, sir"? In his nice, polite voice?

Schmidt turned to the girls, making a frosty attempt at a smile. For some reason they brightened under it. "Miss Batts and Miss Zahner." Steve never did find out which was which. "Mr. Wintress." All of them went through how-do-dos as if this were a silver tea.

Steve said, "See you later," to dismiss Schmidt. But he had to idle over a book while either Miss Batts or Miss Zahner fluttered at the important man—"Your review of that new picture was simply devastating"—while the other one smirked assent.

Mr. Schmidt deprecated, "Thank you." But his shoulders were almost jaunty as he walked out of the store.

The blond shared her admiration. "There isn't anyone with Jo's touch, is there?"

"What kind of touch?"

She withdrew her comradeship. She was hurt if not suspicious. "He reviews motion pictures. He is the only honest reviewer in the city."

Steve didn't care where Schmidt peddled his propaganda or how. "Where's Grasse's office?"

Llewellyn said, "This way, Mr. Wintress."

Steve let him lead into the gloom. He kept his distance until Llewellyn had reached into the cubbyhole and pulled an overhead light. It sprayed on a work-laden desk, old wooden filing cabinets, stacks of books and magazines and a morass of loose papers. Llewellyn flattened himself against the files to admit Steve. He wasn't needed but he lingered. He had something on his mind. "It was you he was meeting at the airport."

"Yes."

"He had the heart attack before you arrived?"

"Yes."

Llewellyn knew better than to ask why Steve had come

66

inquiring for a dead man. You don't ask foolish questions if you are ambitious.

Steve asked, "Had he been sick?"

The youth was startled to a quick answer. "Oh, no!" and then he wasn't sure. "I mean, I don't know—"

"No heart attacks before?"

"Not that I know."

"Have the police been around?"

Llewellyn was cautious. "The police?"

"Asking questions?"

He showed his confusion. "Why should—" It caught up on him and he looked a little sick. He hadn't been told. But he understood. "No." And then he wondered if it were a true answer. There'd always be a few strange customers dropping in, actually interested in books. The police didn't necessarily wear uniforms. He went back to, "Not that I know."

"Don't tell them anything."

The gratuitous advice put Llewellyn back on his feet. The sneer on his nicely shaped mouth was a well-bred one. "Tell the police?" And then the sickness seeped back under his skin. He wanted to comment but he'd been conditioned to accept gospel, not question it. He faltered, "Mr. Grasse was a good man."

Steve said shortly, "He was a friend of mine." Because the anger came up in him when he thought of Albie dying alone, without cause, in the fog, he added, "Someone didn't want us to get together." He didn't give a damn if Llewellyn did pass on the thought to Mr. Schmidt.

He went to the desk and twitched a segment of the papers. It would take a team of men long hours to plow through this mess, longer to make a detailed report. There simply wasn't that much time. The top layer had been disturbed by Mr. Oriole's men, Schmidt had been second. He too must have known discouragement. If embedded in the junk there was a morsel leading to Davidian, the man must be found more quickly than the clue could be.

In the doorway, Llewellyn waited like a flunky. Steve posed a question. "Did he ever come here?"

"Who, sir?" Easier to lose your faith than your breeding.

"Mr. Grasse was to put me in touch with an old friend of mine from Berlin." Steve had no way of knowing how much Llewellyn had heard; the young fellow was as poker-faced as Schmidt. "I flew out from New York for that meeting." The clerk would recognize the importance of such a move; the New York office didn't fly specialists out every day.

"If this man came here, I know nothing of it. Mr. Grasse said nothing."

Albion would say nothing. And certainly Davidian could be expected to have more discretion than to walk boldly into a center. Yet he had called upon Mr. Oriole looking for Steve. The risk would appeal to his sly humor.

"Perhaps he came when Mr. Grasse was out. A small man, small hands and feet—" He went on describing the Davidian he had known and the Davidian who had appeared on Mr. Oriole's porch Monday night.

Uncertainty came to the young man's face. "I don't know. There was a customer—" He broke off. "You should talk to Pam." He walked quickly away.

Disregarding fire hazard, Steve lit a cigarette. He rested himself on the papers which covered the desk.

Pam was the dark-haired one. "It was the funniest thing— odd, I mean. This man came in one afternoon—"

"When?"

"When?" she echoed. "About two weeks ago, I think. Wasn't it about two weeks ago, Lyn? Mr. Grasse had gone to the bank, I remember."

Together they figured. Two weeks stood, possibly a little more, a little less. Steve didn't care that close but he didn't interrupt. He'd asked the question. Two weeks was about right. Steve had still been in Berlin. Waiting for word from Albion.

Pam went on with her event. "He wasn't anyone you'd notice. Lyn and Portia were busy so I took him. We don't bother anyone who just comes in to browse," she explained, "but he didn't. You know, like you this afternoon, you were waiting to be asked and Lyn asked. And I asked him, the funny little man. You could hardly understand him, his accent I mean, and what he wanted was a book of Russian poetry, in Russian, you know, a very obscure book. We didn't even have it listed."

More of Davidian's humor; he'd invent author and title.

"He didn't look as if he could afford to buy a book," Pam continued sympathetically, "but he was very nice and polite. It's the system," she declaimed loyally, "that makes a man hunger for books and not have the money to buy them." With that off her chest, she proceeded. "As he started to leave, he said he wanted to give me something for my trouble and do you know what he gave me?"

68

Steve didn't have the slightest idea and said so. He wouldn't have been surprised if she'd said a map of the Kremlin. Hand-lettered and signed by Joseph Stalin.

"A Russian ruble!"

"Counterfeit." Steve smiled the word.

"How did you know?" Both pairs of horn-rims grew anxious.

He said, "It was a hunch." Davidian up to his old tricks, passing out his calling card. A Davidian ruble. Made by Europe's finest engraver; he'd tell you so himself. Steve was sorry he'd spoiled the girl's story. "Go on, then what?"

She wasn't as glib now. As if she were afraid he was still ahead of her. She spoke defensively, "Well, I'd never seen one before and it was a queer thing for a man to hand you, like a tip, just as if you were in Russia, only tipping is capitalistic and in Russia—"

"I know all about that. Get on with it."

"Well, I showed it to Lyn and Portia and we were all excited about it. Or interested," she defended. "When Mr. Grasse returned from the bank, naturally I showed it to him." She let her bright eyes blame Steve; this was the part he'd spoiled. "At first he was interested too, and then he looked at it more closely and said it was counterfeit."

She could get back to normal now, it was again her story. "He got terribly excited, I mean for Mr. Grasse, because he was always quiet, you know, and wanted to know all about who gave it to me and had me describe the man. He even went out and looked in all the shops around here although I told him the man had been gone, oh, for at least forty-five minutes."

Steve didn't need to ask if Davidian had left any clue as to where he might be found. He hadn't. Through some listening post he'd learned that Albion was seeking him. This had been his thumb to the nose. And Albie had so recognized it; Albion had known that Davidian had waited until the coast was clear before leaving his card. But Albion had come closer than this before sending for Steve.

"The man didn't return?"

Llewellyn said, "We've watched very closely, sir. Mr. Grasse asked us."

"Going home and coming to work. And on the street. Mr. Grasse thought he must be living in Hollywood." Pam said passionately, "I'd know him anywhere. But I haven't seen him."

You won't, Steve said to himself. But this placed Davidian

69

in Hollywood even more surely. His listening post was definitely here; not only had he learned of Oriole's station but also that Frederick Grasse was Albion. It came to Steve, one small check that could be made. He asked, "How many bookshops have we?"

Llewellyn began the tally. "North Hollywood, Santa Monica, one on Jefferson Boulevard—"

Steve said, "Call them. See if this ruble-tipper has been around any of the other shops."

"Now?"

"Now." To the girl, Steve said, "I'd like to see the ruble."

"But I gave it to Mr. Grasse." He should have taken that for granted. "He said he'd give it back." She turned her eyes to the hopeless desk.

Steve ordered, "See if you can find it."

Llewellyn was efficient. He'd completed one call. "He hasn't been in North Hollywood."

"Shove your chair to one side," Steve said. "Pam is going through the desk papers." There could be a message on the bill, one for Steve alone to recognize. More Davidian tricks. "Or anything connected with the man," he told her. "See if Mr. Grasse made any notes." He had an errand of his own. "I'll be back in an hour. I'll tell your girl out front to hold the wheel steady."

The last thing he expected was the complication of Haig Armour out front. There was no way to pass unnoticed. Haig had the effrontery to put on a surprised act. "Why hello, Steve." He gave it the best fancy-meeting-you-here intonation.

Steve didn't play it big. "Interested in books now?"

"Why not? Nice little shop Grasse had."

He tried walking out on that but Haig stopped him.

"I've been looking for you."

"In bookstores?"

"I figured you'd turn up here." Nothing about having the place under surveillance. "Let's go have a drink."

He couldn't say he had a more important assignment. He didn't want Haig's men following. They'd know the Oriole address but he wouldn't lead them there. Schmidt was too suspicious a bastard and too quick on the trigger with his suspicions. Steve didn't intend to finish this job on a lonely beach with a bad heart.

He said ungraciously, "If you insist."

Haig was amused. "We can make it later if you're busy."

"One time's as good as another."

70

They walked out side by side. Steve couldn't manage a word of warning for the blond to pass on to the others.

Together they returned to the boulevard. "Any choice?" Haig inquired.

"That's a laugh."

There were plenty of corner saloons, disguised as jazz joints, yet somehow they shrank out of sight during the shopping day. It was by day a woman's street of hats and dresses and shoes and jewelry, of five-and-tens and movie matinees.

"How about Musso's?"

Haig had named the sole remaining dignity of the boulevard. The old English front with the leaded windows hadn't changed in twenty-five years. Nor had the somber quiet of the *décor* within. At this hour the place was uncluttered and unhurried. They walked past the empty booths to the old-fashioned taproom hidden in the rear.

Haig waited until they had their drinks before starting anything. But he didn't waste time on preliminary social stuff. He stated the fact, "I'm looking for Davidian. So are you."

Steve gave a quick laugh. "You're not going to suggest we pool information?"

"No, I'm not. But I'm going to warn you. You aren't going to get the Davidian report."

If Armour next boasted that he already had the report, Steve would bust him one. No matter what it led to. He was afraid to ask it straight. He made it a taunt. "What makes you think I'm not?"

Haig drank comfortably. "I'm here to see that you don't."

Steve said, "And you don't hold to let the best man win."

"No." Haig passed his cigarette case.

Steve refused, pulled out his own pack. He wished he were as sure of himself as Haig appeared to be.

Haig continued, "I always win."

"That's a pretty big admission. Maybe I could say the same."

"It wouldn't be true." He leaned a steady elbow on the table between them. "Would it?"

Steve didn't answer. Instead he asked, "You did come out here for this job? Not the phony line you gave out."

"That wasn't a phony. But I turned the case over to Timothy Leonard. Would you like to know why?" He was smiling, a dirty smile.

"Spring it."

71

"I knew you wouldn't be sent on anything minor."

Steve shook his head. "You're telling me it was accidental we took the same plane?"

Haig laughed a real one. "You'll be accusing me next of plotting the fog."

Steve stuck to the point. "Accidental?"

"And if I told you we had a tip a man was heading to the Coast to see another man? Nothing particularly interesting in it, your messengers go back and forth constantly. If the tip didn't furnish the name of either man? But suppose I told you that on the plane an astounding human cross-file named Timothy Leonard recognized Stefan Winterich, or Steve Wintress, if you prefer? And where Stefan Winterich makes a personal appearance, something is going to happen?" Haig refreshed his throat.

"What about Feather? She accidental too?"

Haig signaled the waiter. "Two more, please." He stubbed out his cigarette. "I'm afraid I don't know about her."

"You got acquainted damn fast."

It wasn't all in the open. Feather was to be withheld. Steve didn't care, she didn't worry him any. Maybe after all she wasn't a plant; maybe Haig thought she was on Steve's side. That would be one for the books, an innocent bystander and both sides thinking the other had her under orders.

"I don't get it." Steve tasted his fresh highball. This was quota. It wouldn't be funny if Haig pulled the old one of getting the opposition talkative.

As if his side line were mind-reading, Haig remarked, "I thought you fellows didn't drink."

Steve showed his teeth. "We're human too, you know. Some of us do, some don't."

Haig accepted it. "What don't you get?"

"Why you're giving me this pitch." He could play the open-faced hands too. "Why don't you lock me up? You guys can always think up reasons to get rid of your opposition."

Haig said flatly, "I need you. Would it surprise you to know that with all our sources of information, we didn't know until recently that Davidian was in this country?"

It didn't surprise him. "Noooo!" He drawled it sardonically. "The great F.B.I.?"

Haig's mouth tightened. "We've made up for lost time, I can assure you. But we haven't found him. You're going to do that. You were his friend. He believes you're still his

friend, working this deal for him. He doesn't know that you're under orders. You know how to reach him."

Steve pretended amusement. "So I'm to lead you to him and fade out while you pick up the report without interference?"

Haig said evenly, "Frankly I don't give a damn whether you interfere or not. I wouldn't mind in the least getting rid of you for good. I don't even mind if Davidian is a casualty, he's lasted a long time for a spy. All I want is the report." A slight change came across his face. It made him look human. "And I don't want the girl hurt."

Steve waited until he could speak without giving anything away. "What girl?" He didn't want the answer.

"Janni. Janni Zerbec."

He'd half believed her denials of Haig. That was why it slugged him in the pit of the stomach. He had a hard time spitting out the words. "What about Janni?"

"I said it. I don't want her hurt."

Steve tried to fight the sickness that was spreading like poison through his veins. Haig had everything she wanted, power and position, style and brass, money. She hadn't wasted any time; she'd wrapped him up fast. In one meeting? In how many meetings? She hadn't changed any; she was what she'd always be. *Had she given Davidian to Haig?* Were they only waiting for Steve to catch up to the trap they'd staked for him, to catch two birds at once? He wouldn't let them pull it off; this was his baby, he'd set it up. He'd bring it off the way he'd planned it no matter how many angles Haig Armour played.

He heard Haig's voice, the timbre of it. "She doesn't want any part of your deal. Stay away from her."

"Leave her for you?" He couldn't laugh, he tried it.

"You think she'd rather have you?" It was a quiet challenge.

He couldn't see Haig's bold handsome face; it blurred before his eyes. "Okay. Take her. She's yours. I give her to you, no strings." The voice wasn't his own. "But after you've loaded her with minks and rubies and dollar bills and everything her bitching heart desires, remember what I'm telling you now. There's part of her you'll never have. And that part you'll want until you're too old to care, and even then you'll want it. That part belongs to me."

He didn't know how he got out of the booth, out of the restaurant. But he was on the street gulping the air, walking away fast and hard, not knowing or caring where.

73

Somehow with his hat and coat on him. She'd lied, just as she always lied when it suited her dirty little schemes. Just as she was lying about not knowing how to get in touch with Davidian. He ought to go to her right now, slap her with the lie.

God! And what if she had lied? *What's Hecuba to me or I to Hecuba that I should weep for her?*

Nothing mattered except finding Davidian.

2

Early twilight sifted down upon the shiny Christmas crystals and stars and metallic trees. When his eyes and brain began to clear, Steve found he was almost to La Brea. The street was roped off this far up the boulevard. It was necessary to retrace to the corner in order to cross. The Roosevelt Hotel loomed; he rounded the corner and used the side entrance. Only one telephone booth was occupied, and it by a large-size man whose hefty fur-coated dame leaned against the half-opened door. Steve wondered if they were cooking up a story for his wife or her husband. One thing sure, they weren't Haig's hirelings; they'd been here first.

Steve took a booth, put in his coin and called his own room. He didn't expect Reuben to be around but there he was at the other end of the line. Did the kid sit around all afternoon just waiting for Steve to check in? Steve didn't ask; this time it was a break. "How about us dating a couple of gals and making a night of it?"

"Gee," Rube began, then his voice flopped. "Trouble is I don't know any girls in this man's town. Only Feather."

"Stick around," Steve told him. "I'll be there with my little black book." He hung up, put in another coin and dialed again. No one was leaning around the booths; the couple had gone off arm in arm, satisfied with their dime's worth. He answered Oriole's voice, "Wintress here. I'm coming around for some information."

"You will not be long?" Mr. Oriole sounded anxious. "I will wait for you, you understand, but it is that tonight is the Santa Claus parade—"

Santa Claus parade. It explained the streets, the baubles, the colored lights. Steve said, "I'll be there in about thirty minutes. Will that do?" He had to get Rube started first.

"You understand," Mr. Oriole protested too much. "It is not myself. It is that I have promised the children and my wife."

74

"Don't worry. You'll get to see Santa Claus. What I want won't take long." He left the hotel by the same side entrance. There was parade excitement in the air this early. Some particularly eager beavers were spreading their newspapers and blankets for front-row seats.

Reuben was finishing a shave. "What's the scoop?"

"You have Feather's phone number?" The Moritzes were unlisted.

"Yeah. Want me to call her?"

"I'll call. I want you to take the car and pick up my girl." My girl; that was a good one.

"You promoted a car?" Rube mopped his cheeks.

"An old heap. But it's wheels. Janni lives downtown. In a dump but don't let that throw you, she's okay." He explained, "She doesn't have a phone."

Rube had rummaged a scrap of paper out of his coat. A Crestview number was pencil-printed on it. "Janni," he repeated. Well, he'd heard enough about her last night to be curious.

"I haven't time to pick her up, I have to see a man." He wrote her address on another scrap of paper. "Don't take no for an answer. Tell her we're going to have a front-row seat to see Santa Claus." Steve flung out his hands. "Why am I briefing you? That's the first thing they teach you army Joes, how to sweet-talk the dolls. We'll meet at —" He'd go right back there, his head high. He'd have it out with her there. "—Musso's. It's across the street, up a block or so. The car's in the lot in back of the hotel." He dug up the parking stub.

Reuben was slicked up real pretty. And Steve wouldn't have time for a shave. The boy took the keys. "How're you going to get Feather if I've got the car?"

"Feather's going to join us, sweetheart. Run along. Remember, don't take no."

"I won't." Out came the slow grin.

Steve was asking for Crestview before the door closed. Feather might have ten other dates but he doubted it. She didn't react as if she were accustomed to the rush of fellows most girls of her age enjoyed. If she should have Haig Armour plans, Steve would have to convince her that a change was desirable. Someone had to take care of Rube while Steve worked on Janni. He sprawled on the bed while waiting for the Moritz houseman to get her to the phone.

Her soft hello came through.

"Feather? Steve. Look, Rube and I are lonesome." He

75

didn't give her a chance to break in, just kept it moving fast. He had no time to waste on her. "How about meeting us for dinner and we'll take in this Santa Claus parade?"

She was hesitant. "I don't know. I'm not dressed."

At this hour was she still hoping Haig would call? Or did she have to clear through him? "We aren't fancy. Say about seven, Musso Frank's." He wouldn't mention how she was to get there. Let her figure that out. "Okay?"

He barely gave her a chance to say, "All right," before he hung up. He was out of the room at once. He'd have to move fast.

The sidewalks were beginning to jostle. And there were cops all over the place. Steve ducked down the nearest side street and proceeded to Oriole's. The door was opened before he could ring. The parade must be important, Mr. Oriole had washed his face and was wearing a jacket over a clean shirt. He didn't invite Steve into the parlor.

He spoke hurriedly. "This information you wish—"

From the dining room came the quelled voices of youngsters. Steve wondered how many little Orioles were waiting there and if they all looked like Pop. "Where would I find friends in Hollywood? Our friends."

Mr. Oriole didn't believe it was this easy. He began with the bookstore and Steve suddenly remembered Llewellyn and Pam, the job he'd set them on. "Ring them for me."

"The store will be closed at this hour."

"Not until they hear from me."

Mr. Oriole's face drooped but he was obedient. While he put his coin into the slot and dialed, he continued the tally. A record shop, a small café, a magic store. His eyes rounded at an answer to his call. He passed the phone to Steve and stood on one foot then the other.

Steve questioned, "Llewellyn? What did you find?"

"None of the other shops have had our experience."

"What about the desk?"

"Nothing. Nor any notation."

Steve mumbled sounds.

"Is there anything further, sir?"

"Not tonight. Enjoy the parade."

He could hear the smiling condescension. "I'm not going to the parade, sir. I have a committee meeting."

"Enjoy the meet. And thanks for hanging around." He banged up the receiver.

Mr. Oriole continued as if there had been no interruption. "And there is, of course, the popcorn man."

76

Nothing but bad breaks, that pattern hadn't been disturbed. Albion had not thrown away that ruble; 100 to 1 he'd had it in his pocket when he went to the airport to meet Steve. "What about the popcorn man?"

For the moment Mr. Oriole forgot his anxieties. "He has a little cart with glass over and about it to keep the popcorn warm and clean. He pushes the car himself and there is a lantern in it with such a nice yellow light. It is a real lantern that burns, not electric. And a little whistle, such a nice whistle." His smile was nostalgic. "Once I was the popcorn man." He added too quickly. "It is much better the work I do now and this big house."

Steve asked, "Where do I find him?"

"He walks the streets at night selling his popcorn. And meets many people." The small eyes were shrewd. "If his feet get tired, he sets down the wagon on any corner he chooses and the people come to him."

There wouldn't be a much safer way to deliver messages. It didn't sound like the efficient Schmidt; it would take someone before his time, someone with more imagination and romance to invent the popcorn man.

"He is easy to find because of his nice yellow lantern. And the little whistle."

"Yeah." Steve nodded thoughtfully. The dining room was becoming impatient. He hurried. "Where did Albion live?"

Mr. Oriole didn't withhold the address this time. "It is a rooming house."

"Friends?"

"No. Mr. Albion preferred not. It was safer, he believed." Oriole wasn't as sure as Schmidt that Albie was a traitor. He spoke as of a friend.

"Who took over his things?"

"Temporarily it is Llewellyn who is in charge of the store."

"I mean his personal stuff, his clothes, that kind of thing."

"I do not know this. You may ask Mr. Schmidt."

Steve said, "I will. Better get those kids off to the parade." He went to the door, opened it.

Mr. Oriole could smile again. "Always they enjoy the parade. There is Santa Claus—" The smile disappeared as if it were Cheshire. "You understand, they do not believe this superstition," he said carefully. "It is only—" He extricated himself. "It is Hopalong Cassidy and Roy Rogers they wish to see."

"Yeah, kids are all alike." He was sorry for the old boy.

Trying to live up to Schmidt's standards and yet give his children a happy life.

He had time to visit the gathering places, or some of them, and still beat Feather to the restaurant. There were cops all along the boulevard by now, cops and family parties with innumerable children. The adolescents were even more numerous, they paraded on the sidewalks, boys and girls in jeans and bright wool shirts, shrilling cryptic messages to attract the others' attention. The spirit was holiday, Steve hadn't seen anything like it since he was a boy. The spirit was so good it was contagious. He didn't want to be on his gritty little errands, he wanted to be one of these people, just having fun.

A job was a job. He took the far address first. This wasn't one of the clean, shining record stores of the boulevard, it was no more than a hole in the wall, a front. It was open but not patronized. A young man was lolling on a folding wooden chair behind the cash register, reading the evening paper. He looked up at Steve. He didn't rise.

"Is this your place?" Steve didn't like the sullen face.

The fellow flickered an up-and-down glance. As if he'd sized Steve for a plain-clothes cop, he asked with open insolence, "Yeah. What about it?"

Steve gave him more rope. "I'm looking for a guy who's giving out phony rubles."

The smile jeered. "No kid?"

"Has he been in here?"

"Nope." He resumed the evening paper.

Steve let him have it, cold and ugly. "I'm from New York. Mr. Oriole sent me here."

The paper dropped. The fellow was on his feet, stammering something about not knowing.

Steve eyed him. "Now suppose you answer my question."

The slack mouth became voluble, sweat was breaking out on the unwashed face. But the answers added up to a negative. Small wonder. Davidian couldn't have any fun in this dump. Nor would he waste his handiwork on a lout.

Steve said coldly, "I shall recommend you to Mr. Schmidt." He walked out while whey-faced was still stammering about being sorry. It took him a couple of blocks to get back to the crowd's good humor. He should have clouted that one across the mouth when it first opened. It was better to see that the guy was pitched to the lions along with Schmidt.

He had to pass Musso's to retrack to the magic store. The usual dinner crowd overflowed the small vestibule. Steve pushed through to the head waiter. He gave his name for a table for four, watched it written at the foot of an already long list. It would be at least thirty minutes before he came to the top of the list.

He ducked out, threading through the ever-increasing street crowd towards his second goal. It was a poor edition of the boulevard's better magic stores but it was busy tonight. Two middle-aged men, much like junior Orioles, were doing their best to take care of things. Steve waited while Tweedlededum sold false noses to five shrieking teen-age girls. The man was giggling as heartily as the girls. He wiped his eyes with a fat little finger as he turned to Steve. "And now, what can I do for you?" His accent wasn't as heavy as Oriole's.

Steve said, "For a gag, I need a ruble. Do you have any?"

If the man was uneasy, he covered up. "We do not have any real money. Only the phony, you know, stage money."

"I hear there's a fellow in Hollywood making phony rubles. He hasn't tried to sell any to you?"

"No." The man tapped his shiny head and thought some more about it. While he was wondering what Steve was truly after. "No, I have not heard about him." He glanced upward slyly. "I don't think this man, he's very smart. This is America, Mister. Rubles are not wanted here, not even bad ones." He wasn't going to be caught out by any undercover investigator. "Anything else I can do for you? A false nose, maybe?" He laughed as if he'd made a wonderful joke. He was still laughing when Steve went out.

There wasn't sufficient time remaining to check the café; it was past seven. He didn't mind keeping Feather waiting but he'd hate to be pushed down to the foot of the reservation list again. Feather was there, standing just inside the door, trying to peer through shoulders. Steve came behind her and touched her elbow. She swerved a little fearfully.

"Been waiting long?"

She said, "Oh," before she recognized him. She needed those glasses. "No, only a minute or two. It was terrible getting through traffic. And finding a place to park." She wasn't dressed up, just a blue knit and small hat to match, a cream-colored tweed jacket about her shoulders. She'd fluffed her hair a bit, she looked quite pretty.

He said, "Hold it while I check the reservation." He edged through the crowd. The list showed only two names on top of Steve's, plenty of others beneath it. He'd timed it just about right. He reported back to Feather. "Not much longer."

She gave him a quick smile. She would prove tonight that she wasn't afraid of him. "Where's Reuben?"

"Coming. Unless he's already here and holed up in the bar." He doubted it; there'd scarcely been time for a round trip to town, even without the delay of convincing Janni. "Do you want to shove through for a drink?"

She said no, with a glance at the stolid ranks blocking them.

"Suits me." He eyed her. "You're looking very pretty."

She lowered her eyes. "Thank you." She didn't like personal attention, at least not from him.

"Seen Haig today?"

"No. Have you?"

"I had a drink with him here this afternoon. He might still be around."

She perked up on that.

"I suppose this big parade's old stuff to you."

"I haven't seen it in years. Not since I was in high school."

"You don't go for such mundane pleasures?"

She defended herself. "I haven't been here much. I've been studying in New York."

"That explains the hat. The New York touch."

She leveled a glance at him. "You don't like me very well, do you?"

"Because I mention your hat?" He laughed. "Hollywood girls don't use them, I've noticed. Not often."

"You don't," she repeated.

He heard his name called as she spoke. "I'll break trail." By pure chance they rated a good semicircular booth midway in the narrow room. She slid in at the left, leaving room for him beside her. He didn't follow. He sat on the right where he could watch for Reuben. He told the waiter, "We'll have a drink while we wait. Feather?"

She said, "Just a sherry."

"Make mine a Manhattan." He didn't know why he'd gone fancy; devil-may-care to show Miss Prisms? He picked up the conversation. "Let's put it this way. I don't think you go for me. You're afraid. Why?"

"I'm not!" she denied with heat.

"Maybe it's this. You don't go for young men. Not that I'm so young, but Rube is. Most girls would think he was a pretty good shake, nice-looking kid, easy to be with, and if you're the kind who thinks seriously, the family's okay, your uncle said so. Instead of making time with him you play up to Haig Armour, who's old enough to be your

80

father. Why? Because he's old enough to be safe? Or is it an uncle complex?"

She was furious. "I didn't play up to Haig any more than to anyone else. And if I did, you of all people—" Her lips pressed into a rigid line.

The waiter set down the drinks. He was old and splay-footed, the waiters here were all comfortably old. "You must order your dinners early if you do not want to go hungry to the parade." Paternalism was one of the attractions of Musso's. "At eight the lights will come on. It starts! But it will be eight-thirty," he confided, "before it gets to us. Even later."

"As soon as the others get here," Steve promised. The stem of a cherry curled over the rim of his squat glass. It was the night when Janni foraged the jar of cherries that he'd concocted the Manhattans. Maraschino cherries in the rubble of Berlin. He drank and he told Feather, "Forget it. If Haig's what you want, go after him." But you've got competition, Feather; you're pitted against the best there is."

She said thinly, "I don't want Haig. I don't want any man. I haven't time for any man. I have my work." She sounded like a fifth-grader reciting from memory.

And he couldn't tell her what a little fool she was. That work was a cold island on which to isolate yourself, while all the warm, beautiful realities surged by. Because Reuben and Janni were pushing past the barrier.

Janni wasn't expensive like Feather. Her raggedy hair was tumbled, her scarlet dress was cheap, and her coat red, the same red coat. She was lucky to have one coat. But she didn't need sleek grooming; she was the quickening of your heart and the racing of your blood. The throb of your loins. The anger for her which had strengthened him was no more.

Reuben could have let her go over to Steve. He wasn't stupid. He slid her into the booth and himself after her, shoving Feather over to Steve. Steve had sent Rube after her, he couldn't hate the kid for it. He'd known the risk. Rube was young and alive. Steve said factually, "Feather, this is Janni, and vice versa."

Rube said gaily, "Hello, Feather," not a kid out of it to-night. The guy with the best girl, sure of his prowess. "What are we drinking?"

"Make mine Manhattan," Janni said.

For a brief instant her eyes haunted Steve. Or maybe he

was just hoping that the curve of a stem on his glass had stirred her memory too. The silly little phrases that returned to slice the heart in your breast. A jar of cherries that lasted a week or was it two? A jar of cherries and a mean attic room.

The drinks came to bridge the moment, to blot out days which were better forgotten. After the dinner order was given, no memories remained. There was no love or hatred, only a job to be done. Steve waited his turn. He waited until Reuben finished making a good yarn out of his adventures in finding Janni's place. Then Steve tossed it out, as if it, too, were the beginning of a funny story. "What do you think, Janni? Davidian's in Hollywood."

The shine left her face, her eyes became flat jet disks. "You have found him?"

"I'm getting warm. He's been up to his old tricks." He confided to the others. "This is a guy we knew in Berlin. A counterfeiter."

Feather frowned. "Last night you said you did not know him. When Haig Armour asked."

Steve told her, "It wasn't any of Haig Armour's business."

Rube echoed, "A counterfeiter."

"Yeah. Slickest one you've ever seen. A real artist. He made the plates for the phony stuff the Nazis intended to plant on us. Fooled plenty of experts."

"A Nazi." Feather's voice crawled.

"And a Commie too," Steve continued cheerfully. "After the Russians took over, he went to work for them. Getting them ready for their conquests."

Feather's disbelief silenced her. Reuben came to the point. "How could a guy like that get into the United States? What's he doing here?"

"That's what I'd like to know." He was sardonic. "Me and the F.B.I."

Janni flared into the sudden silence, "They can't hurt him. He hasn't done anything wrong. I don't believe what you say!" She hadn't given him to Haig; she was protecting him from both sides.

Steve asked, "What did I say? Not that he is in trouble. There's no law against handing out phony bills that I know of, so long as it's rubles, not dollars. But with the F.B.I. after him, could be—" He let it lie there; maybe she'd change her mind, maybe she'd start considering that Steve wasn't as big a menace as government officials.

The dinners were being placed and you didn't spoil good

food with controversy. Janni laid Davidian aside to sniff over her plate. Reuben didn't care about Davidian anyway, he was out for fun. But Feather continued to worry the story. "Maybe I could find out from Haig why—"

Steve cocked his head at her. "Eat your dinner." Janni was alerted and Steve added, "We'll talk it over later."

They finished the meal in spite of the increasing hubbub of excitement from the street outside. A steady exodus of diners warned of the parade's nearness. Steve waved a bill at the waiter. "Hold our table. We'll be back."

Janni ran ahead with Rube. She could lay trouble aside, you learned that in Berlin. Steve was left with Feather. She might not have been sniffing her patrician nose but she wasn't amused. They reached the street just as the myriad-colored bubbles overhead sprang to radiant light. The voice of the long boulevard answered with a multithroated cheer. The faint sound of a band from Vine Street, blocks below, was an obbligato to the shouting of children. Rube was jockeying Janni into a better position. Steve maneuvered a hole for Feather and himself. Not that she cared, but he liked parades.

The opening was quiet, with a Nativity scene and angel-robed carolers, reminder of the first Christmas before the plunge into holiday merriment. The good humor of march-ers and onlookers alike struck Steve anew. This wasn't a European parade for the purpose of fluffing the ego of a dic-tator or to flaunt the bristle of military strength. It wasn't a New York parade, stage-managed by some junior Ziegfeld, precise as the Rockettes' routines. This was small-town in a big town, kid bands, stream upon stream of kid bands with high-stepping girls twirling batons and twisting brief satin skirts; skinny boys in fancy uniforms blowing loud on their shining horns, beating loud on their drums. This was Western, with silver-decked palominos and cowboys in sil-ver-studded chaps, with trick riders and proud horseflesh and the children yelling for more. It was drums and bugles pacing the quick step, dancers and clowns, and the glaring spots of the TV cameras. The glamour of Hollywood was minor, a number of glistening floats, candles on the icing of a cake. Overhead the little lights beamed red and yellow and green on the silver stars and the shiny Christmas trees, far overhead the true stars were pale in a deep cobalt sky. And Steve saw Davidian.

Only the face, the sharp ferret face wedged between a woman's fur collar and a man's elbow. Peering out eagerly at the show, directly across the street from where Steve was standing. He might as well have been across an ocean and a continent. Separating him from Steve was a solid phalanx of onlookers; beyond, children pressed from curb to ropes, the police patrolling their safety. In the center the river of prancing bands and horses and trundling floats continued its unending flow.

Steve muttered, "Back in a minute," to Feather, not caring if she heard. Janni and Reuben didn't. Steve walked as far as Highland before he was able to dart across to the south side of the boulevard. He retracked then, eeling through the onlookers. It was slow going at best, made slower by the search for one small man. The audience was constantly shifting for better position; there was no promise that Davidian would have remained where Steve had left him.

When he reached that section, he paced more slowly. There wasn't a chance of pushing through to where he could look into faces; he had to be content with unidentifiable back views. By patient moving with the crowd, he managed at last to catch sight of the fur collar. But no thin, shabby man pressed against it now; on either side were gabbling women.

It hadn't been an illusion, Davidian had been in this neighborhood. He was here now, lost somewhere in the mass, peering under some other shoulder. With agonizing slowness, Steve continued on, examining coats and shoes and the backs of heads. He walked all the way to Vine and waited out the combined bands of Orange County before he could cut over to the north side again. His eyes followed the montage of faces across the way as he headed back towards the restaurant. He saw fat and thin faces, dark and light faces, faces from Europe and Asia and Africa, all the American faces, Hollywood faces, but not Davidian's.

He'd forgotten Santa Claus until he saw his face too, the great jolly whiskered saint in his traditional red and white, riding on top of the finest float of all, crying his "Merry Christmas" through the amplifier, while Hollywood snow sifted a benediction over his head. The children and Santa Claus shouted joy to each other. Steve didn't join the chorus.

3

The onlookers broke ranks quickly after Santa's float passed, hurrying to reach their cars, to be first in the clog of traffic. Steve jostled his way through the confusion to Musso's. The three were again in the booth, the vacant place was beside Feather.

"What happened to you?" Rube wanted to know. "We've ordered dessert."

"I thought I saw a friend across the street."

Janni whispered, "Davidian."

"I saw him."

For a moment she was frightened and then she began to laugh. She knew him too well, she could read his failure. "But you could not find him in the crowd!" She slanted her eyes at Reuben and he began to laugh with her. Because he wasn't an innocent or because her laughter was infectious as a parade and ice cream and youth.

Reuben laughed. "Chocolate cream pie à la mode."

Feather's words slit thin and cold. "I'll find out about him from Haig." She actually put a hand on Steve's arm. As if she were sorry for him, as if she wanted to help him.

He covered the hand. He didn't tell her that Haig didn't know as much as he did. "Thanks, lady." Her flesh quivered under his touch.

The old waiter set the desserts. He beamed, "A good parade this year, a real good one. Better than last year." He said it annually. And meant it.

Reuben and Janni were savoring their pie and ice cream. There was no way to separate her from him. It was always tough to get an occupation army out once it was in. Rube said, "We're going dancing at the Palladium. Kenton's there."

"Janni has to work."

"She's taking tonight off." He grinned. "Why don't you and Feather come along?" Big-hearted Reuben.

Steve lied, "I'd like to." He apologized to Feather. "I have a business date."

"It's all right," she assured him defiantly. As if she were pleased that he wouldn't waste time on a dance hall; that he, like she, was dedicated to work.

They broke up in front of the restaurant. He watched Feather round the corner to her car. He watched Reuben and Janni disappear towards Vine. Over the deserted boulevard, the colored lights were darkened, the ropes and stanchions were removed, only the litter of torn newspapers remained as reminder of the brightness of parade time.

The Prague, his last address, was only a couple of blocks away. Steve left the boulevard and walked towards it slowly, as if he were tired, but it wasn't that which made his steps heavy. It was a small café, gimcracked with atmosphere, the usual red-checkered tablecloths, and candles dribbling down the sides of old wine bottles. A fat man with a greasy mustache played a sentimental violin and a taffy-haired lad, who needed a haircut, a balalaika. The music wasn't Prague, it was a musical comedy piece. *My darling . . . my darling . . .* the violin crooned. And the balalaika tinkled an answer, *My darling . . . my darling . . .* Cigarettes swirled a blue fog around the candle flames. Behind the cash register was a big busty woman in a flowered peasant-style dress; her hair was dyed the color of fresh brass. Steve didn't try for a table, he went directly to the women.

"I'm looking for a guy."

She spoke pure New York. "You a cop?"

"Do I look like a cop?"

"Cops don't always look like cops."

"I'm not. That's why I'm looking for a guy. To tip him off."

"Maybe you think this is a bookie joint?"

"He isn't a bookie." He leaned an elbow on her counter. "He's a little guy, thin, dark, doesn't speak English too good. He's been going around passing counterfeit rubles."

She gulped, "Nuts."

"Yeah. Did he hand out any here?"

Words were beyond her.

"To the waiters? Would they mention it if he did?"

"Mention it?" Her tower of brass nodded precariously. "Rubles yet!"

He said, "Thanks," and he went out of the place. Davidian might have been in any and all of these blind alleys but with a different joke.

There remained Albion's boardinghouse. Eleven o'clock was too late to pay a call but he could walk by, if there were signs of activity he might inquire. He hadn't any other lead except to walk the streets looking for the popcorn man. His steps began to take on the rhythm of an old song, abridged to his own needs:

Oh, have you seen the popcorn man, the popcorn man,
                              the popcorn man,
Oh, have you seen the popcorn man
                              who lives in Hollywood . . .

Albion had lived south of the boulevard. It was another of the relic sections of Hollywood, a half-dozen frame houses left behind when business moved in. The address he had been given was the tall house next to the corner. There were signs of life, plenty of them; the parlor lights were bright behind undrawn shades, the voices were loud and merry. In one of the foolish coincidences of the everyday, the radio was singing the same old song of the Prague duet, *My darling . . . my darling . . .*

He walked up to the open screen and he found the bell. The man who appeared smelled of beer. He was just a man, maybe a shoe clerk or an electrician or a cop off duty. He said, "Come on in. Party's not over yet." He didn't wait for Steve to explain himself as a stranger, he held open the screen and Steve followed him into the parlor.

There were several men who might have been the host's brothers, there were women to match, and there was a fat old woman billowing over the best chair. And there was the reason for the party, a teen-age girl who'd marched in the parade. She was still wearing her brief red satin skirt and her soiled, high white boots. Her satin top hat was on the table with the beer. The girl—she couldn't have been more than fourteen, all knobs and angles—was leaping in excited dance steps until Steve's entrance halted everything. Everything but the radio moaning its song of heartbreak.

He began, "I'm sorry to bother you."

The fat woman came out of the chair. Her face was flushed from the beer, one strand of her scant gray hair hung over her ear. "You are looking for a room?" She pushed at the strand but it fell again rakishly over the little fat ear.

He was sorry to bring remembrance of death into this celebration. But death had been here; it was not his doing. He said, "I wanted to ask about a man who used to live here, Frederick Grasse."

The silence was even more silent. These people had known him better than anyone had known him in his last months. They had lived with him.

The man who'd admitted Steve asked bluntly, "Are you from the police?"

He'd never been taken for a cop as often as tonight. "No," he said, "I'm the man he went to the airport to meet. My plane was late." And he asked, "The police have been here?"

"Been here!" The teen-ager wagged her frizzy hair. It was bleached almost white. "We've had tons of them! They keep coming!"

It must have been her mother who spoke petulantly,

"Don't exaggerate, Melba." She had the same rabbit nose of the young girl and whining lines about her lips.

Steve said, "I suppose the police took all of his belongings."

The old lady was suspicious.

"I'm an insurance man from New York," Steve explained to her. "Mr. Grasse was making out a report for me."

Insurance was something she could understand. "You won't find it here," she told him. "They took everything."

"They tore the room apart," Melba exaggerated further. The soft song had died, some noisy cacophony had replaced it making all of them shout. No one turned off the radio; they were accustomed to its competition. Melba rounded her eyes. "Do you think he was murdered?"

"Melba!" her mother complained. "Where do you get such ideas?"

"Well, the police don't tear a room apart when a man dies of heart failure, do they?" Having made her point, the little girl grabbed a cookie and crunched it between her crooked teeth.

"The kid's got imagination," her father said proudly. "And she's got a point," he told the roomful, gesturing with his beer bottle. "Do the police move in when a man dies natural? When Pa had his heart attack, did the police move in?"

They'd been over this time and again, making the same points, the same rebuttals. It was in their faces. The old woman was the only one not amused by the untoward excitement. She glared at them but she didn't say anything. When she looked at Steve there was a spit of fear behind her washed-out eyes.

Steve asked her, "I suppose you've rented the room?" It wouldn't do him any good to see it, the police would have taken anything he could want.

"I rented it the day after," she defied him. "Lucky. Very lucky."

The police had known from the beginning it wasn't heart; they'd autopsied and known; they'd torn up the room and left it for renting the next day.

He said, "Thank you," and turned to go. If they only knew how to tell him. They'd seen Albion daily while he was hunting down Davidian; they'd seen him while he fumbled for the trail, when he'd been cold and then warm, hot, when he'd reached sight of the goal. He tried again, "Did you see him when he left that night?" Had he known he'd been marked for the sacrifice? Had he believed he could be safe long enough to meet Steve? He must have believed that, he'd reached the airport.

The woman slapped at the irritating wisp of hair. "I saw him." She'd told it so often, it was by rote. "He came home from the bookstore about six-thirty and changed his clothes. I met him out there in the hall. I asked him if he was going out. Just making conversation. He told me he was meeting a friend at the International Airport. He said the plane might be late because it was already foggy but he had his key with him. I lock up at eleven."

Steve nodded. Albion had been alone, she'd mention it if there'd been a friend with him. She'd answered all these questions before. "Do you know what time it was when he left?"

"I don't watch the clock." She was tired of him, she wanted him to go away and leave them alone.

But he kept on. "Before dinner or after?"

The shirt-sleeved man, he must be a son, said, "Before I got home. Because I asked Grammaw, I asked, is Fred home? I'd brought some beer and I thought we could have a beer. I don't like drinking alone. Sometimes we'd have a beer together before supper. But he'd already gone."

"So you had it alone," the wife said sourly.

"So what's a beer? You think a beer makes an alkie out of a man?"

Steve said, "Thanks." No one seemed to notice. He went out into the night. The radio and the loud voices and the smell of beer followed him up the street.

Somewhere within this small section of the city's map, Davidian was waiting for him. Why couldn't Davidian have sighted him when he sighted Davidian? The man must know he was in town; why no message? He could answer that one. Because Davidian was under Steve's own orders; the contact must be made Winterich to Davidian, not the reverse. It was that extra measure of safety. But Davidian was too cute not to figure out a way to reach Steve without making contact. Unless he had and Janni was deliberately withholding it. Or unless Davidian had sold him out.

Oh, have you seen the popcorn man . . .

A man who knew those walking the streets of Hollywood. No bobble of a yellow lantern. No smell of hot popped corn. Janni and Rube were still dancing or they'd parked somewhere in the car Steve had promoted. The boulevard was deserted, the shop fronts dim, the office buildings empty shafts. Gusts of music rattled from the jazz bars. Steve turned in at the dull lobby of the hotel, started across its emptiness to the elevator.

But it wasn't empty. The man on the settee laid aside the morning edition which had been masking his face. He said, "I've been waiting for you." Just an ordinary guy, Steve's size, wearing a beaten brown hat and a trench coat as old as Steve's. It took a second look to recognize Wilton.

"What for?"

"There's some men who want to see you."

Steve started by him. "Bring them around. Ten cents a look."

Wilton halted him. Not violently. With no more than a disinterested finger upon the sleeve of his coat. "I'd come if I were you."

Steve took out his cigarette pack, lit one while he thought about it. "That's the way it is?"

"That's the way."

He hunched his coat. "Let's get it over with."

Tonight it wasn't the big hearse. Just a sedan, nothing shiny, nothing you'd notice.

Steve said, "I'll sit up front. I get lonesome."

Wilton gave a nod. You couldn't get much out of this guy.

"Don't you get tired running errands for the brass?"

"Don't you?"

It was a fair retort, both of them were working stiffs, neither called the shots.

"What does Armour want now? Didn't he get enough this afternoon?"

Wilton didn't bother to answer. He carried along on Sunset to the Doheny hill, on down to Santa Monica Boulevard. When the Beverly Hills city hall loomed a white and golden fairy-tale tower, Steve tightened. He could take questions, not a lockup. He relaxed when Wilton directed the car straight ahead, following Santa Monica across Wilshire, continuing on past dark woods. And on, until he drew up in front of an inconspicuous motel. It had some Spanish name on it.

"Haig's moved," Steve commented.

Wilton said nothing.

"You can run out of dough fast putting on a front." He didn't feel as flip as he sounded. He could crack Wilton one and take off. But it would necessitate getting out of town

90

fast, and he couldn't leave town until the job was done.

Wilton stood beside him on the sidewalk. "Number ten's in the rear. It isn't Armour wants to see you."

Steve didn't move. He hadn't considered it this way. "Suppose I don't like this?"

"You don't have to like it. You'll save yourself trouble if you take it."

Their eyes met on even keel. Wilton was right, he knew he was right, and he knew Steve understood. There were plenty of ways to get a guy who didn't co-operate.

"Coming?"

Steve dug his hands in his pockets. "What do you think?"

Their steps were solid on the concrete walk leading to the rear right bungalow. Wilton rapped on the door. The man who opened it was a narrow dark young fellow in a blue suit. "Hello, Cal. Mr. Wintress?"

"Who else?" Steve returned insolently. The two men waited until he walked inside. But no lock turned behind him. He stood in a miniature living room. There was another guy on the couch against the further wall, heavier set, balding; his suit was gray. Not an elegant tailored job like Haig Armour's gray, just a suit like the blue one, or Steve's own.

The blue suit gestured, "Mr. Wintress, Hale."

Hale said, "Sit down, Mr. Wintress. You know Ferber and Wilton."

He didn't sit down. He didn't have to. Ferber returned to his straight chair backed up to the window. Wilton took another chair, swung it around to protect the door.

Hale said, "We're having a beer. Join us?" The beer cans were on the low table, moist beads stippled on them. A paper sack had crumpled to the floor. These were temporary quarters.

Wilton said, "You might as well sit down, Wintress. You'll be more comfortable. And you might as well have a beer. Or do you drink only with the brass?"

The three men were a triangle hemming him in. He lifted his shoulders, took the place they'd left for him, the one comfortable chair. He might as well take the beer as well. "Okay," he said. "Get started." There was probably a recorder under the couch or in the curtains. They wouldn't get anything on him.

"We're curious about Frederick Grasse's death," Hale began.

"You think I killed him? I got witnesses. Ask Wilton. Top brass ones."

"What makes you think he was killed?" Ferber had a college man's voice, smooth, educated.

They knew the answer. "The Feds don't get curious about heart failure."

Hale asked offhand, "Why was he rubbed out?"

"You know more than I do."

"No," Ferber denied in his quiet way. "We don't. We don't know why."

Steve pushed up in the chair. "For God's sake, you think I know why? After making a trip all the way from New York to see him?" They knew damn well he had nothing to do with Albie's death. Their informers would have reported how important it was for Steve to see Albion. "Why the hell don't you find the killer and ask him why? Why figure me in?"

"Because," Hale said, cracking another beer for himself, "you and Grasse were tied up with another man. A man who has disappeared."

Steve said, "I don't know anything about it. I came out here to see Grasse. He was dead before I arrived." They couldn't change his story.

"You knew he didn't die a natural death."

"For God's sake," Steve said wearily. "I guessed it. Haig Armour wouldn't be interested if he had."

Ferber put in, "What's happened to Davidian?"

Steve didn't answer.

"Grasse is dead. Davidian is missing. You're left. Top dog."

He didn't like it. Not even with the knowledge that they were only playing him, figuring he might spill something.

Wilton announced without interest, "Even Commies have their little spats."

He wanted to walk over and push his fist through Wilton's face. "So Grasse was a Communist? Do you have to ask a guy to take a loyalty oath before you call him a friend?"

Hale ignored that. He remarked, "You know what I think? I think there was a slip-up in plans. I think Davidian and Grasse were bumped off too soon. Before you got your hands on the report."

He lost his temper. "Davidian isn't dead!"

Wilton said offside, "He does know more than we do."

"He isn't dead." But the cold hand on his neck wouldn't

92

lift. Like Haig, they were so damn sure of themselves. Davidian wasn't dead, not yet. Davidian was too experienced to be dead. He wouldn't let it happen until he turned over the report. And he wouldn't turn it over to anyone but Steve. He spoke quietly, in control of himself again, "I saw him tonight. At the parade."

They didn't believe him. They had a dossier on Stefan Winterich, a story of betrayal and death; they wouldn't believe anything he said.

"And he turned the report over to you?"

For the record Steve said flatly, "I didn't get to talk to Davidian. He got lost in the crowd. I don't know anything about a report." If Hale had checked with Armour, he'd know damn well that Steve knew about it. But it was different talking across a Musso table with Haig and talking to a hidden wire recorder. One which could, by a carefully arranged accident, fall into Schmidt's hands. Divide and destroy. Let Schmidt destroy Stefan Winterich; keep Haig Armour's manicured hands clean.

"Don't you?" Ferber let the legs of his teetering chair clack down hard on the linoleum floor. But his voice was still nicely modulated, Harvard grad. "You don't know that Davidian escaped from Berlin, the Eastern zone, that is, carrying in his head the war plans for Soviet expansion through Western Europe? You don't know about Davidian's photographic memory, considered as fabulous as his draftsmanship? You don't know that he managed to carry a few notes with him to bolster that memory? Or that heads fell like walnut shells in East Berlin when Davidian came up missing?"

"Maybe I heard something about it." It wouldn't have been possible to be in Berlin and not hear about it. And they'd know it. When it was discovered that it wasn't Davidian in the t. b. ward but just another scrawny guy who hardly resembled him, everyone in both zones heard plenty of Davidian.

"But you didn't hear that he was writing a report of what he learned while engaged in certain work for the Reds?"

Steve told the truth. Not that they could recognize it. "That didn't leak out." The clamp of censorship saw to that.

"You didn't come to L. A. to grab that report?"

"You mean he hasn't turned it over to his American pals?" Steve jeered.

"It's possible he doesn't mean to turn it over to us,"

Ferber said. "It might be he plans to sell it."

To the outfit with the biggest bank roll. They could believe this yarn. Davidian's reputation as a dirty little spy was well established.

"You can stop worrying," Steve scorned. "I'm broke."

"There's only one thing worries me," Hale stated. "Where's Davidian?"

Steve laughed.

"Something's funny?" Wilton demanded.

"Yeah." He laughed some more.

"Hand us a laugh."

"You've got it." He gave them the same needle he'd used on Haig, it always worked. They were so damn proud of their organization. "The great F.B.I. with all its terrific brains and stupendous resources can't find one little guy. And they think I can."

He let his glance pace over the three of them. "I'm a stranger here, remember?"

Ferber said quietly, "It might be easier for an old friend from Berlin to find him. A guy whom Davidian might believe to be his friend."

He didn't like Ferber. "That's the way you see it."

Hale rested his heavy hands on his knees. "There is something you'd better know, Wintress. If anything happens to Davidian, we're picking you up for murder."

Anger flooded him. "Like that!"

"Like that." Hale jabbed a hand towards the door. "Take him home, Wilton."

Steve was on his feet. "No wonder Haig Armour has such a big-shot reputation. He can railroad anyone who gets in his way." He hit all of them with his buckshot words. "You've been following me around. Okay. Just keep on. Stick closer to my tail. Because if anything happens to Davidian, I want witnesses that I didn't do it. Witnesses almost as good as I've got for Albion's murder." He started to the door. "I don't know how in hell you figure I'd want Albion out of the way—" In anger he'd used the wrong name, the private name. But there wasn't one of the three who didn't get it. "If I'm here for the reason you've dreamed up, God knows I'd be an idiot to get rid of the one guy I needed to find Davidian." Somehow he managed a degree of dignity. "Frederick Grasse was my friend."

Ferber said almost sadly, "In your decalogue, Wintress, a friend is a friend only as long as he conforms to orthodoxy. You have no friends."

Steve circled their faces; Hale was an old man, Ferber young, Wilton between; in detail each one was separate but each wore the same face. One that was steady, purposeful, and merciless. He wondered fleetly if there were real men behind the faces or if the organization chose only men with these faces. He'd wondered the same of his own organization. There was plenty he could say; plenty he'd like to tell them. Hale, the sledge hammer; Ferber, the knife; Wilton, the punch to the jaw. He held his tongue, walked past Wilton into the night air, damp and fresh from the Pacific, a few miles further west. In silence he proceeded on to the car, silence broken only by Wilton's steady heels behind him and the riff of cars passing on this quiet stretch of the boulevard.

He maintained the silence on the ride back to Hollywood. He had nothing to say to Wilton nor Wilton to him. Each was no more than a cog in his particular pattern. If they changed sides, they would be unchanged as men; if they were on the same side they would enjoy comradeship, not enmity, but neither man would be changed.

At Sunset and La Brea, Steve said, "Let me off anywhere along the line."

"Wherever you say."

"I don't want the F.B.I. delivering me to my hotel this time of night. There might be talk."

Wilton said no more, he stopped at the next corner. Walking was better. Streets were peaceful in the early morning hours. Steve passed Oriole's. He was too tired to report, much too tired to wait while Oriole routed Schmidt out of bed to listen to the night's developments.

The sift of street light through the window of his room showed the shape of Reuben in his twin bed. Rube said, "I'm not asleep. Put on the light."

"I don't need it."

Reuben said, "You must have made out. Coming in at this hour."

"I told you it was business." He didn't want to ask but the kid was waiting for it. "How did you make out?"

Rube stretched for a cigarette, the match made a small cone of light. "Pretty much of an all right." He wasn't fooling anyone. "That Janni's a swell kid, isn't she?"

"Yes." It stuck in Steve's throat.

"Swell dancer."

She ought to be. She'd danced her way out of the rubble, she who could dance even in rubble. A kid in a scramble of

95

kids begging from the conquering heroes. A beggar kid, with matted hair, dirty rags on the stink of her body. But she'd danced. Fire and joy blazing out of her black eyes. That and hate; he hadn't recognized the hate at that time. He'd been a dumb, good-natured American like Reuben. Fifteen years old and she didn't look more than twelve. He'd thought she was twelve when he tossed her a chocolate bar and a couple of cigarettes. Until she came to him, put her mark on him. Because she'd picked him to get her out of the muck.

"I want to explain something," Rube said solemnly. His skinny shoulders hunched against the headboard of the bed. "I wasn't trying to make out with your girl. But she said she wouldn't come unless it was with me. She said you wouldn't care." In the half-light he searched Steve's face for a clue. "I feel like a heel, Steve. You've been regular with me. But the way she said it—I can't explain exactly—but it didn't seem as if it was important. She made it kind of a part of the fun of the evening."

"I didn't care," Steve said. "Skip it."

"I'm not saying it right."

Steve laid his clothes neatly over the chair before he came to bed. "I understand, Rube. I know Janni. I know she can make things sound however she wants them to sound." Trivial, gay, terribly important, terribly sad. While her devil within mockingly observed the effect. "But she was telling you the truth. I didn't care if she was with you. It's not that beating me. It's the conference I've been in."

He'd made it right. Reuben's guilt faded out of his young voice. "I said I'd call her tomorrow."

"Okay."

"I told her I'd take her to some broadcasts."

"Sure." If Reuben kept her busy enough, Haig Armour couldn't be hounding her.

"She's been here almost a year and she's never been to a broadcast."

Reuben wanted to talk about her, it was that way when you were excited about someone. That way when you loved. A long time ago Steve had had to give up that small but sometimes essential luxury. It didn't matter to him any longer. But he wished to Christ that Rube would shut up about her.

96

IV

HE DROVE TO ORIOLE'S in the morning. Not that it wouldn't have been simpler to walk the few blocks but he wanted to reassure the poor old guy that his shabby car was okay. He hadn't announced his intention to drop in. He hoped he could catch Mr. Oriole alone.

Mr. Oriole was chewing on a cinnamon bun when he answered Steve's ring. Crumbs were caught in the rough of his chin. A coffee-stained napkin dangled from his belt. He wasn't surprised to see Steve, but he apologized, "I am sorry." He was trying to hide the bun in his large soft hand. "I did not get to bed early. So a late breakfast."

Steve said, "Take your time."

"You would perhaps join me for a cup of coffee? And cake? My wife bakes excellent coffee cake."

Steve started to refuse. And then he didn't. Mr. Oriole was sensitive and Mr. Oriole was helpful. A man's feelings were worth more than a few minutes' privacy. Furthermore, the coffee Steve had gulped at a corner white-front hadn't been the last word in breakfast. He said, "I haven't had any good coffeecake since I left Berlin."

The woman was embarrassed but the two small boys, and they were replicas of Mr. Oriole, were only curious. Mr. Oriole said, "My wife, Ingeborg. She does not speak English much. And two of my sons, these are named Jim and Jack. The other children work on Saturday mornings. Very fine sons. Five of them."

No wonder the woman looked old with six men to do for. She rubbed her hand on her apron before extending it to take Steve's. It was a light hand with baking. Steve resented the intrusive doorbell, not only because he was afraid it spelled Schmidt. The smile left Oriole's fat cheeks as he plodded to answer. It might have been that Schmidt too had called for a private confab.

Steve didn't follow him. He beamed at Mrs. Oriole and

97

stuffed away another wedge of cake. "You're okay," he murmured. "You've put me back on my feet."

She spoke gently, in her halting accent. "A man needs a woman to cook for him. You have no wife?"

"Not yet."

"Do not wait too long." Her eyes crinkled. "The best ones go first."

"I've found that out."

Mr. Oriole returned, undraping the napkin from his pants. "It is Mr. Schmidt," he said hopelessly. "He is waiting for us."

"Dandy." Steve finished his coffee. "Thanks, Mrs. Oriole."

She took his hand again. "You remember what I tell you."

"I'll remember." They exchanged a blessing.

Schmidt was stiff in the best chair, crease in his pants, starch in his collar, briefcase at his polished heels. He was in good humor. "Good morning, Mr. Wintress. You have news?"

"I have." Steve lit a cigarette. "The cops picked me up last night."

He'd smashed whatever dream Schmidt was harboring. Behind the lenses the eyes lost their luster. "For what reason?"

"They didn't give a reason. They asked questions."

"Concerning?"

"Concerning Albion's death."

"Why are they intervening in this? For what purpose do they meddle?" The thin nose was pinched with white anger.

"They don't go for executions. This is a free country."

"Yes." The word was a snake. But Schmidt didn't proceed into dialectics. He would know Steve could recite the speech as well as he.

Mr. Oriole ventured, "This is not a nice development."

"They want to mix me up in it."

Schmidt considered. He would be pleased to offer them Steve but he didn't dare. There were higher authorities protecting Stefan Winterich. "You were not here."

"That's what I keep telling them."

Schmidt said slowly, "I do not understand this."

"They made it clear. Albion and me—and Davidian."

Schmidt lifted his panes of glass. "They can't find Davidian."

"Can you?" It was in the open now, Schmidt's resentment of an outsider being injected into his kempt affairs.

Steve faced Schmidt coldly. "That's why I'm here." He

didn't elaborate. "I was warned that if anything happens to Davidian while I'm in town, I'll be pulled in for his murder." An idea stirred in Schmidt but Steve quashed it. "I'm telling you to warn all of your eager beavers that if anyone lays a hand on Davidian while I'm in town, it will be not only the end of your job, Schmidt, but all the way down the line. Got that?" He waited for an answer.

It came under pressure. "I understand, Mr. Wintress."

Schmidt would be a threat from now until the end of one or the other of them. If for nothing but this humiliation before the subordinate Mr. Oriole.

"You do not expect them to reach Davidian before you do, Mr. Wintress?"

He'd been waiting for Schmidt to slash. "No, Mr. Schmidt, I don't. If they were on their toes, they would have had him before now. He's been leaving his calling card all over Hollywood." Oriole quivered but Steve wasn't giving him away. "Albion knew."

"He did not tell me!"

"He also knew the value of silence in some matters." Steve went on factually, "I'll get the Davidian report for you. I simply want to make sure in advance that none of your staff makes any more mistakes."

"You may be sure." There was open hostility behind the glinting eyeglasses. He quoted himself, "We wish only to co-operate, Mr. Wintress. We realize you are working against time with Haig Armour and his Gestapo after the same material." As far as Schmidt was concerned, Wintress would have to prove himself the miracle man. "May I suggest again that the girl could be made to talk? I understand there is a lover in the Soviet zone."

Schmidt was behind the times. "You refer to Janni Zerbec?"

"I do."

"I told you once I'd take care of her. That stands."

The lips were dangerously thin. "Very well, Mr. Wintress. I understand."

Steve accepted the insinuation. He didn't move until Schmidt dropped his eyes. "Good." He quit the parlor then, knowing Oriole would follow to the front door, to be certain he was out. He'd have that long. He let Oriole open the door for him but on the porch he turned back. Schmidt couldn't overhear even if he had his ears against the parlor drapes.

"I couldn't find the popcorn man."

"He went home early." Mr. Oriole was nervous. He had a session ahead with Schmidt. He didn't want Steve on his neck too. "Because of the parade, you understand. He sold out his popcorn early. But tonight he will be around. Perhaps on Ivar in time for the intermission?"

"I'll look for him." He swung away but was halted by Oriole's soft voice.

"The services are this afternoon for Mr. Albion. You will be there?"

"No one told me."

"Mr. Schmidt intended to mention it. He had so many things on his mind."

"Where?"

"In Santa Monica. At four o'clock." Mr. Oriole read off the name and address of a funeral parlor.

"Why Santa Monica?"

Mr. Oriole said, "His family lives there. It was his home." He was mildly surprised that Steve didn't know.

"You'll see me." Steve clattered down the wooden steps. Schmidt had deliberately withheld the information. It would have been hard for Steve to explain to either side why he had not been present. He would be present.

He drove the heap back to the hotel, left it in the back lot. Reuben was making like a crooner while he polished his shoes. He cocked an eye. "When did you join the early birds?"

"It wasn't for fun. What about Janni?"

"I'm taking it easy waiting for noon. There's a public phone at her place. She's going to be downstairs at noon for the call."

Steve lounged on the foot of Rube's bed. "I've got a suggestion. You don't have to like it or take it but here it is. Call her at noon but meantime I'll start on downtown. You tell her I'm on my way and to be ready. I'll bring her back to you and you two can do the studios while I go about my business. Then we can all meet for dinner."

"Okay," Rube said. What else could he say?

"I've got some things to talk over with Janni. Might as well do it while I'm taxiing her to you. Save time."

Rube was quiet. "She's not mixed up in this thing of yours, is she?"

Steve went at it carefully, "She's not mixed up in anything with me, Rube. And she doesn't intend to be. You don't have to worry about Janni." He continued, taking it slow, "But

100

the man I'm here to see roomed at Janni's when he first came to L. A."

"The counterfeiter?"

"He's not in that business any more. Except as a gag. He never did it for profit, Rube, only for a favored position. You don't understand. You couldn't. Not the way you've lived. You don't know the provocations of Europe."

"Maybe not." Maybe yes, he'd been in Berlin. "He's a friend of Janni's?"

"Not particularly. She knew him." Through Davidian's friend, Stefan Winterich. "She'd help any refugee to get started in an alien land." Unconsciously his voice toughened. "She knows where Davidian is. She won't tell me."

"Why not?" The quiet, unanswerable question.

"I wish I knew." He repeated, "I wish to Christ I knew." He waited but there were no more questions. "See you soon."

The sky and the air were balmy, the way California should be. A picnic day. If the world and you were young. Neither would ever be again. Because the grime of Europe was embedded in your very bones, you couldn't forget reality in these endless streets of white houses, green handkerchief lawns, flowering vines in brilliant winter bloom. The decay of Janni's neighborhood was more closely attuned to this era of destruction. He drew up before the woeful house. Maybe the world would have been a better one if it had lived in eternal summer. Even this dump was gay with red blossoms climbing its scaling walls, redder flowers billowing about its tired porch.

He was early. He sat in the car until twenty past the noon hour, giving her time to get back to her room after the phone call. He didn't want to surprise her. He took it easy on the stairs. As he headed down the corridor on second, he had to step aside for a painted, angular blonde in a garish green dress. She was in a hurry but she slowed her teetering heels for his attention. Incongruously she twitched his mind to Feather.

He took the last flight and strode to Janni's door. There was the usual nothing on his first knock and he knocked again. He expected the old woman's evil eye at the door's opening but it was Janni herself standing there, barefoot, her purple and pink bathrobe about her, her face softened with sleep. When she recognized him, she said automatically, "Get out."

He pushed the swift-closing door and was inside the room. She was alone. "Why don't you call the police?"

She wouldn't, not to protect him but out of fear of involving Davidian. He lifted her hand off the knob and banged the door shut. The impact trembled the walls.

She threatened, "Get out of here."

"Didn't Rube tell you I was coming?"

"Rube?" She pushed at her scalloped hair. And then she came suddenly awake. "What time is it?"

"It's past noon." Steve helped himself to a chair. "Get dressed. He was to tell you I was on the way to pick you up. I'm to deliver you to him."

She yanked open the door. "You will wait outside while I dress."

"I'll wait right here. It'll give us a chance to talk things over."

"There is nothing for us to talk over."

He settled himself, lit a cigarette. "Get dressed. You're keeping Rube waiting."

She glared but she banged shut the door. Again the walls shivered. She ignored him, walking to the stained sink beside the stove, splashing soap and water. He kept quiet until she was toweling herself.

"Have you seen Davidian yet?"

She walked back to the wardrobe, swept aside the limp cretonne curtain and eyed her few dresses.

"You're going to see him today. This is the day you give him his dough."

After a brief moment she removed the hate of her eyes and carried her clothes over to her bed. She dumped them there, turned her back on Steve, and began to dress.

He grinned, "I know plenty, sweetheart."

She said viciously, "Don't call me sweetheart."

"A colloquialism which slipped out. Pardon, Fräulein Zerbec. Where do you pay off?"

She perched on the edge of her cot to slide the sheer nylons over her exquisitely long legs. He'd given her her first nylons. The other kids had been happy with chocolate. She'd been as hungry as the others but she'd wanted nylons and a red lipstick.

"If you know so much, find out." She dropped the kimono, slipped the narrow black dress over her head.

"I'll find out if I have to stick to your tail every minute of this day and night." He made the words count. "I don't want to go that far."

She smoothed the dress over her breasts, down her small

102

rounded hips. "You are a louse," she said serenely, but her eyes were jagged with anger.

"You've picked up a few colloquialisms yourself, sweetheart."

She began to brush her hair with fierce strokes.

"Haven't you learned by now that Davidian wants to see me? That I'm the only one who can peddle his report?"

Carefully she put down the brush. "Why do you go on with it?" She spoke quietly. "Do you honestly believe you can double-cross the party—and live?"

He didn't figure in her fears; it was Davidian alone. He said curtly, "Think it over. I'm meeting you and Rube for dinner."

"And your fancy blond?" Her moment of weakness was gone. She stood at the smeared mirror, coloring her mouth. "La di dah!"

"Maybe this will help you decide. The F.B.I. picked me up last night for a little talk. They've warned me if anything happens to Davidian, I'm the fall guy." He got to his feet. "Nothing's going to happen to Davidian while I'm in town."

She caught up her red coat, her cheap black purse. "You are leaving soon?"

"As soon as I've talked with him."

They shouldn't have looked into each others' eyes. Too long a moment. She said unsteadily, "We must not keep Reuben waiting any longer."

There were no more words until they were just another man and woman in just another car trundling along the busy streets of the city. He had to reach back into memory for the words that raised her question.

"Where do you go?"

When the job was done? "Wherever I'm sent."

"Back to Berlin?"

"Why not? A job's a job."

"You have not changed." She spoke not with regret but stating a fact.

"Did you expect it?"

"No." There was no more than a faint shading of doubt. "You made your choice. And you are stubborn."

"Let's say logical. Sounds better."

"However you say it, you would not admit to being wrong."

His laugh jeered. "You say I'm wrong."

"Before I came to your country, I accepted that you could be right. That you were right when you believed you had picked the side of ultimate victory." She shook her head. "Now I know how wrong you are. And I do not understand how you can believe otherwise."

He said, "I don't get you, Janni. There's only one reason you wanted to come to the U. S. and that was to pick up some of those gold and silver chunks that pave the streets. And those refrigerators and swimming pools and big cars and fancy clothes and all the rest of it. What have you got? A slum almost as bad as you were raised in. Bargain-basement duds. Ten-cent perfume. A job that doesn't pay you enough to eat right, a job that only the hopeless would touch. That's your land of promise. Empty promise. You'd have done better to stay in Berlin."

"No," she said and she was so very sure of herself. "That is where I know you to be wrong. Not even if I could have those gold and silver things in Berlin would it be better there. What you hold in your hand does not matter. There is something more important. To be free."

"Free!" He snorted. "Free to live like dirt. That's good?"

"It is good, Stefan, to be free to live as I will. To go to a dance or to a movie or to a church or to stay home; to read whatever I wish to read, to speak in any way I wish to speak, to think as I wish to think. Day or night to do what I choose, without fear." She was like a torrent. "No papers! It was many weeks before I lost my fear when walking home from work at night, very late, I would spy a policeman. I would begin to search for my papers." She illustrated, scrabbling into her purse, and then she smiled, happy as a child. "Until I learned to remember—no papers!"

He grimaced, "And you think it's right for the rich bitches to have Beverly Hills and you Skid Row?"

"I am free to move to Beverly Hills."

He denied it with a laugh. "There's a little capitalistic device known as the economic system. Boiled down it says that the guys at the top aren't going to let the guys at the bottom come up. They're free to keep you down below. And you're free to stay there."

"You know better." She wasn't angered. She was almost patient with him, she spelled it out primer-clear. "I am free to go to school. And the school is free. It is called adult education. When I am a stenographer I will not remain on Main Street. When I am a good stenographer I will move to Beverly Hills. If I want to move to Beverly Hills. If I do

104

not, I will not have to move there." She studied him somberly. "You cannot understand, Stefan, because you were born to freedom. You do not know what it means always to be a serf, always to live in fear of the masters. I was born to the Nazis. When they were gone, there were new masters. There was no change, only a different name. It was worse than before possibly, for they were alien masters; they did not even speak the language of their serfs. You were born with freedom from fear. This I never knew for myself until I came to your so big and beautiful land. I had been told but I did not know how to believe it until I myself knew it to be true." Her lips tightened. "And I do not understand you and those like you who would destroy this freedom. For what? For your own ugly reasons."

"You wouldn't be blabbing about freedom if the cops were chasing you. If the F.B.I. was on your tail."

"The criminal must always be afraid, yes. And the traitor." The word curled from her tongue. "In my country it is not only the evil men who live in fear, it is everyone, the good and the honest and the innocent. Everyone who is not corrupted by the master race. Whatever name these masters call themselves."

The car was moving along Hollywood Boulevard and Reuben would be taking her away from him. She wasn't the girl Steve had known in the Berlin gutters. She was Janni but she was someone new.

She stated, "It is for this reason I will not deliver Davidian to you. I will not risk his freedom."

Steve didn't say anything. He left-turned and drove into the lot. In her stilt heels she came to his shoulder. Berlin street kids who were raised out of wartime garbage didn't rise up tall and serene as did California youngsters.

He steered her into the lobby. From the nearest banquette a shined-up Reuben jumped to greet them. "I was about to give you up." He beamed at Janni. "Hello."

"It is my fault. I oversleep. I apologize to you." She was soft now, a woman with woman tricks, not an adversary.

"Don't you apologize," he told her. "I was just afraid this guy had decided to keep you for himself."

"That is not possible."

You could take it any way you wanted; you could skip it. "I've got another date," Steve said. With a dead guy. "There's a little place on Cahuenga. The Prague. Meet you there about seven."

"Okay." Any dump was okay with Reuben. As long as

he had Janni. He was already skipping her out of the
lobby. If Janni's eyes had sharpened at the meeting place
named, Steve couldn't tell. It could have been a trick of
the light.

2

He reclaimed the car and drove out Santa Monica Boulevard, shoddy save for its Beverly Hills beauty spot, to the
city which named the highway. The house of dead men was
the usual mansion, this one something out of Colonial Old
Spain. The surrounding homes of the living shrank humbly
away from its elegance. For the living, crusts; for the dead
who couldn't taste it, icing cake. Steve walked up a gracious
flower-bordered walk and into the marble foyer. He removed his hat on entering; it was that kind of atmosphere.

The office attendant was a corseted matron in black satin.
Her blue-white hair was waved with wig precision, the
rouge on her pink powdered face was too bright. The corpse
wouldn't be painted any fancier.

Her unction didn't hide the coarseness of her voice. "May
I be of assistance?"

"I'm looking for Frederick Grasse's family."

She tiptilted a watch brooch. "The funeral won't be for
more than two hours, Mr.—"

"I know." He bottled his impatience. "It is the family
I'm looking for. You have the address?"

The fishy eye she protruded at him turned him into a
shyster. She had a good reason to be wary, this elegant dump
wouldn't care for the police background of Albion's death.

He forced a sad, sweet smile. "I am an old friend of
Frederick's. I just arrived in town from New York and
learned—" He let his hands spread his regret like treacle.
"I hoped I might be of some comfort to his mother. Fred
and I were boys—" He kept slathering it on because she
liked it that way. He even pulled out a handkerchief and
honked his nose.

The dame was still dubious. "It isn't usual, Mr.—"

He side-stepped the name again. "Years ago—" A word or
two was all needed, she supplied the remainder out of the
echoes of experience. And it finally worked. She retreated
into her small office while he waited in the doorway, snuf-
fling into the handkerchief. She consulted a card file.

"Mrs. Grasse lives on Seventeenth Street." She recited the
house number.

He repeated it as if it were a dirge. "I can't thank you enough." He recalled he was a stranger. "Is it far?"

She figured. "About twelve blocks." She tapped the card. "I have been loaned a car."

That cheered her. He wasn't just a bum, he could borrow a car. "Just drive out Wilshire or Santa Monica. The house is south of Wilshire." Across the tracks, her nose inclined. Not too far across for this outfit to grab the business.

He restated the thanks and moved fast. Before her dubiety reheightened and she thought of calling the mortuary brass, or staking him out for a cop. There should have been a cop around. But they wouldn't expect any of Grasse's friends to show up this far ahead of the funeral.

On wheels it wasn't far to Seventeenth Street. The Grasse bungalow was yellow frame, midway in the block, indistinguishable from the other bungalows in the neighborhood. It wasn't shiny and it wasn't art but it was tidy. There were the usual red flowers clustering about the steps and against the house. Early-blooming poinsettias were tall against the windows.

Steve parked in the nearest space, up the street. The Grasses had other callers. Or the clan had gathered. He knew nothing of Albion's family, only that there was a mother. Albion was forever speaking of his old mother, with no apparent reason he would bring her into a zone of conversation, and, after a sentimental moment, permit her to leave. Conscience? Or was it only by holding fast to her hand that Albie had the courage to stand up to a hostile world?

Steve walked back to the house, up the walk and up the shallow steps to the door. So many walks and steps and doors in so many worlds. Behind the doors a home. For him never a home. A room in a flea-bag, a final resting place in a trash can in some alley. Alleys were the same all over the world, as were the little houses. He pushed the bell and heard the answering chimes.

The woman who appeared was tall and sparse, her black dress serviceable, not new for the funeral. She had a thin, sharp face, tearless behind her gold-rimmed eyeglasses, her hair was beginning to gray. She waited for Steve to speak.

"Mrs. Grasse?"

"I am Miss Grasse." She didn't ask him in. She held the door almost with defiance, certainly with rejection. This wasn't the usual mourning house open to all who came bearing the drooping leaves of sympathy.

He felt impelled to explain himself. Not to force entrance,

107

but in exoneration. "My name is Steve Wintress. Your brother and I were friends."

Nothing softened in the lean woman. If anything she became more rigid.

He tried harder. "In Berlin. I hadn't seen him in five years. I was looking forward to it. When I arrived, I learned he was gone."

She didn't welcome him, but she said, "Come in." Out of curiosity concerning a part of her brother's past?

The hallway was small and sunny with a yellow plaid wallpaper. It was uncluttered; there was an unframed modern mirror, a three-legged mahogany table beneath it. On the table, in the exact center of a square of white linen, a silver vase with green branches was placed.

She led into the living room at the right, another small room and on any other day a pleasant one. The furniture was old but the flowered covers were clean, the wood polished, the mantelpiece unadorned. There were minor etchings on the walls, one of Washington Square with the Arch a slant at the righthand corner, one of the fantasy skyline of Manhattan, one of a river and a young apple tree. Frederick's nostalgia for a more serene past?

Miss Grasse said, "Mama, this is Mr. Wintress. He says he knew Fred in Berlin."

Mrs. Grasse rose from a straight chair, a chair which didn't belong to the room. It was maple, decorated with some unidentifiable small white-paint flowers. Probably from a breakfast-room set. The mother was her daughter twenty, thirty years hence. As tall, as spare, more gray, more lines on the skin. But there were deeps in this face that would never be in the spinster's. Mrs. Grasse had borne life and death.

"You knew Fred?" There was German in her speech, a long time ago.

Steve took her hand and he felt shame. He hadn't come as a friend; he'd come to ask questions. Determined on answers.

With increasing disapproval, Miss Grasse said, "My sister, Mrs. Knott, and her husband, Mr. Knott."

These were plain people; the sister could have been older or younger, she was softer and more round but these qualities didn't allay the hostility in her. The husband had the tired look of a man who had worked hard and honest for long years and small reward. He, too, was hostile. The only warmth was in the dry hand of the older woman.

It was she who urged, "Sit down, Mr. Wintress," and she indicated the big flower-covered chair. The company chair. The brother-in-law left it and put himself between the two Grasse girls on the flowered couch. His white collar was especially white against the weathered red-brown of his neck, and his stiff Sunday shoes were heavy on his feet.

"We bury Frederick today," the mother said. There was no outward grief, whatever agony curled her heart because she buried her son was covered by her flat black bosom. Nor was her mourning dress new. "You were his friend?"

"Didn't he ever speak of me?" He and Albion had been friends, if ever he'd had a friend in the organization. Albie talked of Mama away from home; at home wouldn't he talk of his friend?

"Fred didn't live here," Miss Grasse stated. Her diction was coldly precise.

Her sister added to it. "He lived in a room in Hollywood."

"It was his business," the mother explained to Steve. Perhaps the stranger would believe this; the others would not. "He worked very hard at his business. He could not live so far from it." She wasn't a soft woman, she said it without emotion, "He was a good boy. He came to see me." She dared the others to doubt it.

Steve repeated, addressing her alone, "He spoke of me? Steve Wintress?" Because of the sisters he couldn't say, "Of Stefan Winterich?" Because their enmity was too near the surface.

"Fred didn't mention his friends to us," Miss Grasse said. "We didn't know his friends."

Mr. Knott made it clear. "We didn't want to know his friends."

They knew. They knew Fred's business and they were good citizens all. They despised. Only the mother. She knew; she would have been told, over and over; she would have been told with throttling anger, with acid spite. The disgrace of Fred. But he was the son she had borne and she was old and had wisdom. She could wash his sins with pity.

"He was too young to die," she said. Tired, gray Albion was too young to her. Was it because he was a man, small of stature, amid tall, stony women that he had compensated by taking a little unnatural power to himself? There was always a reason. For every one of them a reason.

The mother continued, "He did not tell me he was sick. I scolded him because he works too hard. He is thin and no

109

good color in his cheeks, but I did not know he was sick. He would not worry me."

The other three exchanged eyes. They knew Fred hadn't died from sickness; they knew the police wouldn't question and re-question about a sickness. When Steve was gone they'd tell the mother again, barb it into her heart. While he was here, they couldn't. They were respectable, too respectable to mention the police before a stranger.

"He came to see you recently?"

"Every week he comes," she said proudly. "On Thursday. Every Thursday without fail. It is the night of Marguerite's bridge club." Two against Marguerite. "I give him a fine dinner. Dumpling stew. It is his favorite ever since he was a little boy. Dumplings." She put the passion out of her voice. She wouldn't make dumpling stew again. Marguerite would eat for health, whole wheat and fresh greens. "He ate too much. Because it was so good."

"He didn't mention I was coming to California?"

"He didn't bring his friends here," Miss Grasse stressed grimly. "He didn't talk about them. We didn't want to hear about them."

"I'd written him I was coming." He hung on as grimly. If only he could speak alone to Mama. "I hadn't seen him in five years. A reunion."

"It is good to see old friends," Mrs. Grasse sighed. "I do not remember if he spoke of you."

And the break came. There'd been so few, Steve deserved this small one. The bells chimed. Miss Grasse went to answer; it was safe, she left her sister and the husband on guard. No one spoke. The two on the couch waited tensely as if they feared the ring meant another of Frederick's friends or again the police. Mama Grasse didn't care; she mourned Absalom, her charity covered the why and how he had betrayed them.

There was crisscrossing of voices in the hall, young and old, female and male. Aunt Gertrude and Uncle Nicholas, Cousin Barbara and her husband, and Aunt Anna and Cousin Willie. The little room was overfilled with too many people and their words. But under cover of the confusion Steve could speak privately, in this moment when the Grasse sisters were trapped by the relatives.

He said to the mother, "He planned to meet me."

Her pale blue eyes flickered. "You are the one?"

He pushed ahead quickly. "Was there no message for me? You have his things?" The police would return mementos to the next of kin. They had released Albion; they wouldn't retain the belongings.

"Yes." The hesitation was too long but the sisters continued to be cornered by weeping Aunt Gertrude. "There is no message, nothing." She saw his refusal to believe, because her eyes like Albion's could see. And because Steve called Frederick friend, among his own who had rejected him, because she grasped for one kindness to her boy who had died alone, unwanted, too soon, she said, "I will show you."

She put her heavy-veined hand briefly on his wrist. He started to follow her but Miss Grasse's voice whipped across the room. "Mama!"

The mother's voice was strong. She knew Marguerite wouldn't make a scene, not before the relatives. "I will show Frederick's friend the fine lace shawl he brought to me." Her bedroom was the first beyond the living room, a warm, rose-colored room. There were framed pictures on the wall, family pictures. Three little girls in stiff hats and high-buttoned black and white shoes, two little boys in sailor suits, unreal as cartoons. Steve wondered where the other children were now; he didn't ask. Children were born and they died. She had opened a long bureau drawer and from tissue paper lifted out a folded black lace shawl.

Steve remembered. "I was with him when he bought it. In Berlin." The first time he'd heard about Mama. He touched the delicacy of the fine lace. And he remembered the aged man who had sold it, the furrows in his pallid cheeks, his blackened teeth. He remembered how the old man had held it in his withered hands before he could let it go.

She unfolded it. "See? How big it is!" Her voice was powerful. "It was much too fine for me." As she spread it on her rosy satin bedspread, she was pulling open the small drawer of her bed table. Her voice went under her breath. "This is what came from his pockets." While Steve touched the keys, the license case, the half-roll of mints, she spoke up loud again. "He was a good boy. He was never in trouble. Never!"

And Steve's fingers closed on the ruble, folded so small to escape attention. Not to be thrown away, for Frederick had preserved it; not to be shown to the shame of the good sisters. Steve unfolded it, his back to the woman. She wasn't watching him, she watched the door.

"He could not give me so much as Marguerite, no. She
111

with her fine position, a high school principal she is, for ten years now. He was not so successful."

No message save that Albion had carried it as message, the proof that Davidian was in the city.

Her voice lifted, "Ah, Gertrude! My shawl, you remember this fine lace Frederick brought to me from Berlin?"

Aunt Gertrude blocked the doorway. She mourned, "Always so good to you, your son."

Softly Steve closed the drawer. Miss Grasse's nose quivered behind her aunt's heaving shoulders.

The mother said, "His friend was with Frederick when he bought the shawl for me."

Miss Grasse didn't believe. She didn't know what Steve wanted here but she knew his coming wasn't honest. Her eye was trained to spot excuses.

He said to Mrs. Grasse, "I must go. Thank you for your kindness."

She was a little fearful. As if, in his leaving, he was taking away another part of her son. She took his hand and pressed it. "Come again to see me. Thank you for coming today. Thank you."

Had Albie spoken of Davidian, perhaps a funny story to make her laugh, about a little man who made money and who was hidden in the open streets but no one could find him? No more questions. Miss Grasse was at his side until he was shown out the door. She remained on guard in the doorway until he was beyond the path and out the sidewalk. Her silent mouth was repeating, "We don't want to know Frederick's friends."

3

On the corner of Fourteenth Street there was a superdrugstore and supermarket. On impulse, Steve swung into the parking lot. He took the drugstore, found a phone booth and called Feather's number.

The precise voice of the manservant wasn't certain that Miss Talle was available. Before investigating, he was insistent on the name of the person calling; he'd been trained to preserve the Eldon Moritz privacy. He was worth every cent of the three or four hundred a month he'd demand.

Feather came on the phone. She said, "I have only a moment. Haig is waiting for me."

"Have you found out anything?"

"Oh yes." She sounded pleased.

112

"When do I see you?"

She was hesitant. "I don't know whether I can get away."

He told her flatly, "If you have a date for cocktails with me, you can get away." Either she was without any experience or she didn't want to get away.

She hesitated further. "Y-yes."

"I'll meet you at five. Wherever you say."

She didn't say anything but she was there, he could hear her faint breath. She might be consulting Haig.

"Well?"

"Could you make it at six? It may be difficult."

"Six. But I can't stay long. I have a dinner date." Tonight he wasn't going to drag her along. "Where?"

"The Beverly Hills."

"I thought the point was to shake that guy?"

"Oh yes, he's stopping there," she remembered vaguely.

She was the dumbest girl he'd ever met; no one could be that dumb. "Well, where?"

"The Beverly Wilshire?"

She wouldn't know any dumps, only chromium-plated *bistros*. There wouldn't be any dumps in Beverly Hills. He'd buy her one drink. "Don't be late," he said and hung up. That one would be wasted money. But he couldn't miss any bets. She just might not be Haig's girl.

When he left the booth he realized he hadn't eaten since breakfast. There was time for a sandwich. He sat down on an upholstered stool at the soda fountain, ordered a cheese and coffee. The sandwich came fresh, wrapped in wax paper. He ordered another, and, lured by a shiny brown-and-cream illustration hanging on the mirror, topped it off with a chocolate soda. He hadn't had a chocolate soda in years and it was good. It was like being home.

And then it was time to put in an appearance at the farewell to Albion. Not for Albie's sake but because both sides would speculate over his absence. In their respective myopias they wouldn't consider he might stay away in protest against furthering the ancient ugliness of gathering about an empty rotting shell, a custom perpetuated out of superstition and greed. Albion was gone, a part of infinity. He might even be a part of blessed infinity, he'd made mistakes but the Divinity wasn't the party. You could err; you could, if you had to, hug grievous error, and be forgiven. God could forgive Albion his mistakes, God and Albie's mother.

There were plenty of cars around the funeral home. He

was late, the macabre festivities hadn't begun but within there was a sizable audience. Not mixed. Schmidt and Oriole and Frederick's friends were on one side; on the other were relatives and the family friends. On the outskirts was the law. He recognized Hale's jaw line and Ferber's shoulders. Wilton was further offside where he could check each entrance. Were they hoping Davidian might show? Steve didn't join any group; he took a doorman's position on the opposite side from Wilton. He'd only gone into his folding chair when the immediate family appeared and the man who must be the minister. Mrs. Grasse hadn't veiled her face, her shoulders were straight and her chin; she wouldn't weep. Not for an audience.

The minister spoke briefly, without spirit, he might have been rented with the hall. He was safer with the words of the Lord; his voice strengthened as he read from his book:

> *Have mercy upon me, O Lord; for I am weak:*
> *O Lord, heal me; for my bones are vexed.*
> *My soul is also sore vexed:*
> *but thou, O Lord, how long?*

He was too young to have known Frederick Grasse; had the Lord guided him to the Psalm? Or was it the mother?

> *Depart from me, all ye workers of iniquity;*
> *for the Lord hath heard the voice of my weeping.*

There were hushed steps of more late-comers. Two heads turned, Steve's and Wilton's. There was no need, Haig Armour and Feather didn't hide in the rear. They moved down the short aisle until they were directly behind the family party. Feather couldn't have known she was coming to visit the dead; she was dressed for cocktails in a cap of violets, a spray of them at the collar of her blue suit.

> *Let all mine enemies be ashamed and sore vexed:*
> *let them return and be ashamed suddenly,*

the minister intoned as he closed the book. He didn't try a eulogy, merely a brief prayer for a man who had been and was no more. The murmur of *Amen* came feebly from both sides. No one wept.

It was over and Haig Armour was moving up to the family. Anger spurted into Steve. Armour couldn't be permitted to invade the mother's privacy at this time. Part of the anger could have been his own shame but Steve moved rapidly. And vainly. Feather stood in his way, cat-eyed, smelling of violets. "I want to tell you—"

In that moment, Haig reached Mrs. Grasse. Steve set Feather aside. "Hold it." He didn't bother to see how she took it; he reached Haig.

And he heard the rich voice, properly subdued. "May I express my sympathy, Mrs. Grasse? I knew your son a good many years ago. I had hoped to see him while I was in town."

Steve wasn't needed. The watchdog sisters had closed in and the impresarios of this affair. Mrs. Grasse had only the same words, "He was a good son," and she was conducted away.

Haig turned and looked into Steve's face. If he was chagrined over the brush-off it didn't show. Steve said sardonically, "You were an old friend of Fred Grasse?"

"Hello, Steve. Maybe I knew him."

The mourners were filing out. Schmidt was interested. And Wilton. Neither came forward.

Steve said angrily, "She's decent. Call off your hounds."

"I can't hurt her. Nothing can hurt her further." Haig's jaw was squared. "She might like to know that there are some who aren't willing to condone murder."

He hadn't seen Haig angry before. Maybe it was the presence of the assassins, the hypocrites, mouthing amens. Steve demanded, "And you think you'll find a killer by heckling her? She doesn't know his friends or his enemies. Miss Grasse doesn't allow them in the house."

"You've been there."

"Yes. Unlike you, I was an old friend of Frederick's. Like you I hadn't seen him for a long time. And hoped to see him while I was here."

Haig said, "Maybe you did see him."

"Meaning what?"

"There was time enough. While you were looking for your unknown pal at the airport. Time for more than a few words."

Haig's boys hadn't accused last night. Haig hadn't outright before. It rocked Steve but he hung on. "He was dead when I was on the plane. With you."

Haig said nothing.

"You know damn well he was dead before I got there." They weren't going to saddle this murder on him, no matter

115

how much Haig would like it that way. "The police know. They released the body, they know when he died."

Haig quoted, "The tolerance of the body to certain alkaloids is different in different men. They can't be certain whether Grasse got his before he went to the airport or later."

The attendants were working around the edges of the auditorium, cleaning up for the next show. They wished the two men would carry their argument outside. Feather had drifted to the door, as if she didn't want to hear what they were saying.

Steve's fists ached from their clench. "You'll have a hard time hiring witnesses who can put us together. I came here to do business with Frederick, not to kill him. I can prove that."

"Not on the witness stand," Haig said smoothly. "You wouldn't dare go on the witness stand and reveal your business with Grasse."

That was it. Rage ate at him, knowing they could do this to him, knowing he couldn't make testament of the truth of the matter between him and Albion. Even if they couldn't prove their case, and they couldn't without perjury, they could tie him up long enough to make him worthless on the job. Haig had many ways to win his victory.

Steve whispered, "You bastard."

Haig said, "Don't worry. I don't believe the police will bother you for a few days yet." He moved with the taunt, towards the girl.

Steve waited until they'd gone. When he came out of the place, the pitifully small cortege was driving slowly away. Haig and Feather were advancing to a Cadillac roadster. Ferber and Wilton idled by a plain black sedan as if concluding desultory conversation. Schmidt and Oriole duplicated the performance by another sedan. Steve knew what they were all waiting for. The number-one pigeon. He had no choice. He moved down the walk and joined Mr. Schmidt and Mr. Oriole. It couldn't be news to Ferber and Wilton that he belonged in that category. They'd had his friends tagged before now.

Schmidt asked, "What had Armour to say to you?"

He didn't have to answer. It was none of Schmidt's goddamn business and it wouldn't hurt to tell him so plainly. Nor would it hurt to speak up. "He wanted me to understand that this doesn't close the file on Albion."

"So?"

116

"He's still trying to put it on me. He's capable of having me picked up for questioning. To keep me from reaching Davidian. If that happens, you're going to have a hard time explaining to New York why I wasn't given proper protection."

Schmidt didn't move an eyelash.

"If that happens," Steve pounded it, "you're going to get me out of it fast. If you have to turn yourself in as the killer."

Schmidt inclined his head. The smile on his lips wasn't nice. It was Mr. Oriole whom Steve had frightened. He would have to pick the victim, arrange for proof. Even if he had to turn himself in. Schmidt wouldn't be touched. He was the brainy kind, safe until Steve could undermine him at headquarters. Unless something happened to Steve. His insolence was icy. "Don't worry, Mr. Wintress. We will take care of you."

Steve propelled the question. "Who did kill Albion?"

It didn't disturb Mr. Schmidt. "We are working on that, Mr. Wintress."

Steve didn't shove in the man's face. He simply walked on to the car and drove away. Neither Armour nor Schmidt was worth his blowing his top. He wasn't here to fight big shots. He was here to get the Davidian report.

He should have insisted that Davidian pick a safer locale. But the little guy had seen too many American movies or heard too many tales of eternal palm trees and orange juice. Or was it that Janni was here? Davidian wasn't a man you could drive; Steve had had to have his co-operation. And what was the difference? There were outfits working in every city, Des Moines or San Francisco or New Orleans, name any of them. There was activity in even the small towns.

You couldn't outrun danger, not when you were in the business that Albion and Davidian and Steve were in.

He remained on Wilshire into Beverly, parked the old crate a block away and walked back to the hotel. There was nothing cozy about this lobby; it was as big and glittering as a movie set. Feather wouldn't be early. Time for a phone call.

The phone rang on and on in an empty room. Reuben and Janni would find out he was late when he didn't show up on time for dinner. They wouldn't care how late he was. The call hadn't been to find out if she'd gone to the room with the soldier. It didn't matter to Steve if she had.

117

He left the booth and found the cocktail lounge. It was crowded and noisy, high-class noise, Beverly Hills brand. He had a straight one standing at the bar and returned to the lobby. She wasn't very late. She was still dressed up like a cocktail-hour girl but she didn't play the part. She stood timidly by the revolving door, looking out myopically into the lobby. Steve went to her.

She fumbled, "I tried to be on time. But Haig insisted I have a drink with him before I dropped him at his hotel. I thought it was better. He was angry."

He guided her elbow back towards the fancy bar. The head waiter found them a sliver of space; it didn't take him long to bring a sherry and a weak highball.

Steve asked her, "What has he got to be angry about?"

"This man. The funeral—" She didn't want to continue. "He was murdered. Haig thinks you—" Her eyes scuttled away from him. "You didn't. You were on the plane. But—"

He said sourly, "They couldn't pin it on me but they could hold me too long. What about Davidian?"

She wasn't listening. "Is Haig really F.B.I.? He says he isn't. He says he's a lawyer with the Department of Justice. But Eldon says—"

Steve told her, "He's been an important Federal man for years. What did you find out about Davidian?"

She admitted, "Not very much."

"Haig won't talk?"

"I don't believe he knows. He seemed to be trying to pump me as much as I was pumping him." She seemed embarrassed. "As if he thought you might have confided in me."

If that was a come-on, he ignored it. "He doesn't know where Davidian is?"

"I don't think so. Only that he's in touch with this girl— Janni." She breathed hard against his shoulder. "I know I haven't found out much for you. I'll do better tonight." She was too eager, as if she had to convince him that she was on his side, not Haig's. "We're going to have dinner with him at the hotel. Eldon and Elsabeth and me. And Eldon is going to help me. Eldon's very good at things like that."

Steve said, "My God, did you have to rake in your whole family?"

"Was it wrong?" Her lip fell. "I wouldn't have only I thought—" Her shoulders hunched tremulously. "I mean I thought because Eldon knows everybody, he might know—"

"He couldn't possibly know the man I'm after," Steve said. "Davidian's not a movie star."

118

She caught his wrist. "I'll find out something tonight. I promise you."

"I'll give you a ring." He put a bill on the table.

"After dinner. I'll go home right after dinner." She didn't want him to go; she was fine-strung as a race horse. Her mouth was opening to spill a further delaying action. For what purpose, he didn't know.

He got to his feet. "I'll ring you after dinner." He swerved away. He was threading through the tables, almost to the door, when he noted Eldon Moritz sitting alone, almost directly opposite to where Feather was now alone.

It wasn't the first time he'd wondered what cooked with Eldon Moritz. But it was the first time that it bothered him sufficiently to wish that he weren't already too late for his appointment at the Prague. He'd have liked to join the man for a few presumptuous questions.

It could be that Eldon was only keeping an avuncular eye on his wife's niece and her odd companion. It could be but it wasn't. Not the way Eldon was casting a calculative eye on the girl. Not the way Feather reacted to men old enough to be her uncle. It didn't necessarily have to be a thing between the two. And it was this riding Steve as he steered Oriole's old boat over to Hollywood. There was the matter of Haig's interest in Eldon Moritz, they'd gone chummy fast for a couple of professed strangers. You could never know who was undercover these days, it added to the hazards of what once had been a comparatively simple occupation. One item stood out with clarity, with Feather sandwiched between Haig and Eldon, she was as trustworthy as an adder.

4

The small parking lot attached to the Prague wasn't very popular on a Saturday night. A few cars stood forlorn in the angular shadows. A slovenly boy ambled out of a wooden kiosk to take thirty-five cents from Steve in exchange for a yellow ticket.

After the lonely lot, the café was pleasant. The mustached man and towhead boy were making sounds of music. Through the candlelight Steve spotted Janni and Reuben against the wall. He headed for them, ignoring the beckoning eye of the brass-haired woman at the cash register.

"Sorry to be so late."

119

Reuben and Janni were already eating something Hungarian and their salad greens were strong with garlic.

"We did not expect you," Janni said complacently. She'd cleaned up somewhere—in his room?—she looked scrubbed.

"I said I'd be here." He told the waiter, "Bring me the same." He put his elbows on the table. "When I say I'll be somewhere, I'm there."

"Ha," she mouthed. She was looking for trouble.

And he wasn't in any shape to take it. "What does that mean?"

She slanted her black eyes. "It means, Ha Ha Ha."

"Skip it," Rube murmured.

"Why should I skip it? After those many times when I have waited on the corner, and waited, and waited, for the very dependable Herr Winterich. Ha Ha."

Why this? For God's sake why? She'd kept the past out of it so far, brutally so. Why drag it in tonight? Was she striking out of fear, fear that his delay meant he'd caught up with Davidian? So he'd kept her waiting sometimes, so he'd had to cut appointments without warning, it was over and done with. She'd known he wasn't a free agent.

She shoveled in another mouthful. "And so," she explained to Rube noisily, "when I make an appointment with Herr Winterich, no longer do I expect him. Maybe he will come, maybe not. Who knows?" She licked a bit of gravy off her finger. She didn't say, *Who cares?* It was implicit.

Reuben tried to quiet the waters. "How was your day, Steve?"

"Just dandy." The waiter set a bowl of potato soup in front of him. "I went to a funeral."

She stopped eating.

"The guy at the airport."

"Was your friend?"

"Yeah." He didn't explain why he'd denied him heretofore. To Janni he said, "You remember Frederick Grasse." They'd had him to supper, he'd furnished the schnapps.

She remembered too well. "Albion. He brought you a pair of shoes. American shoes. He is dead? How?" She cut the word like a whip.

"Heart failure."

Over his shoulder the brassy woman called, "Ah," as if she'd been searching for Steve. "I have news for you."

He didn't tip her off to silence. He preferred Janni to hear the news, whatever it was. "Yeah?"

"But it is Bona who should tell you. I asked questions."

120

She waved imperiously to one of the waiters. It wasn't the one attending their table but it could have been. They were all of a type.

"Bona," she said, "this is the man who asked, you know."

Bona twitched his mustache. "It is like this," he began. The other waiter moved in, snatched away Steve's soup dish and replaced it with the goulash. Bona glared his comrade away.

"Wanda was asking about the ruble." Wanda was the woman nodding her glittering pompadour.

"Where did you get it?"

"This I am telling you." Bona wasn't going to have his moment sucked away by undue haste. "I am in the kitchen waiting for the order to be served and the talk turns to Russia. Quite naturally, you understand. There is at the time a dishwasher, a starved dog who works cheap, you understand, because he can eat his fill."

Janni began mopping her plate vigorously with a lump of bread.

"But this man says he is in possession of rubles. This I do not believe. He dries his hands and his arms and he proves it to me." Bona took from his hip pocket a wallet. From it, with care, he extracted the slip of paper. "This one he presents to me."

He allowed Steve to handle it.

"When did he work here?" Steve passed the bill to Janni, let her see for herself. Bona tried to figure without success. Wanda thought it was maybe a month ago. She wasn't sure. She didn't keep records on cheap dishwashers.

"You don't know where he lived?"

They didn't.

"His name?"

"Jake. Just Jake."

The ruble came back to the waiter. He was folding it when Steve said, "It's a phony."

"How?" The man's face fell apart.

"Counterfeit."

Bona didn't believe. He examined it on one side and the other and then he put it away as if he suspected Steve of pulling a fast one. Steve said, "Thanks for the information," to the disappearing apron.

"You're sure?" Wanda frowned.

"I'm sure. Makes them himself."

She didn't follow the waiter, she trailed back to her own corner.

Steve began to stow away his goulash.

"So?" Janni was furious. "He works as a dishwasher to get enough to eat."

"Maybe. Maybe for some other purpose."

"He works as a dishwasher," Janni said heatedly. "He is working, not making money."

"Who said different?" Steve finished his plate.

Janni dropped her anger while the waiter brought the dessert. But before he was out of earshot, she returned to the fray. "Why do you make trouble for him? Asking questions of these people? Getting all of them to spy on him?"

Steve said, "I wouldn't have to if you'd tell me where he is."

"I have told you—"

"It doesn't matter any more," he cut in. "Feather's getting the dope for me." He gave meaning to the lie by a look at his watch. "Remind me to call her after dinner."

Janni disbelieved but she couldn't deny. She thought she alone knew the way to Davidian yet she couldn't be sure. Because Steve knew her so well, he could be amused by the act she began to put on. A light raillery against Feather as an opener, followed by a mockery of Steve for being led along the garden path by a simple girl who didn't know enough to open her umbrella in the rain. For the main show, a biting scorn of Steve, who could slump so low from an established reputation as a huntsman to be forced to depend on misinformation from a stupid animal like Feather. She threw in the implication that it must be Steve's declining powers as a male which could make him interested in such a milk-and-water specimen as Feather.

As always, Steve let her perform. When she broke off to suck the last of the chocolate from her spoon, he tried a point of his own. Janni knew more of local conditions than he. "So she's young, untried, an amateur, I'll grant you. But her uncle is Eldon Moritz."

It was a good try. Janni stopped pretending. It appeared that this was news to her. Unpleasant news. She asked indifferently, "Who is Eldon Moritz?"

She knew who he was all right. She'd recognized the name without delay. But Steve gave her the full answer.

"He's a movie big shot, lives in a comfortable twenty-nine-room cottage up Benedict Canyon, complete with swimming pool, butler, unlisted telephone, everything you've seen in his movies. That's where I'm heading for tonight. To get my information in an easy chair with a good highball, not

122

in some crummy hall room with a gun in one hand and a dollar bill in the other."

She said viciously, "You don't know what you are doing. You are a fool. But you have always been a fool." She was making words, nothing but words. Because she had no way to stop him from going to Feather. And she was afraid of Feather. She spat, "You trust any *halunke.*"

"No," he said deliberately. "I learned better than that. A long time ago."

Reuben wasn't enjoying this. He was trying to act as if he weren't there but he couldn't go on endlessly drinking out of an empty coffee cup.

Steve dropped Janni. He said to Rube cheerfully, "How about ordering a brandy and another round of coffee. I've got to make that call."

He had to pass the counter to get to the phone. The woman called to him, "Mr. Winterich." He hadn't given her his name. "You understand I had no idea this dishwasher was important." They were all so fearful of making a mistake, even an inadvertent one. "I am in the kitchen so little, I don't even know who is hired."

He told her, "It isn't important. It could have been but it isn't."

Some of the worry lines went out of her powdered face. "If I'd had an idea—"

"Sure, sure," he assured her. Tell it to Schmidt or Oriole. He wasn't interested. He shut himself in the booth and called Feather. She'd reached home; she said she was alone, the others had gone to a movie. Her voice sounded farther away than Hollywood to Beverly. But he gathered she had something to tell him. Something she called important. He couldn't miss any bets. "I'll be there within the hour."

The woman was still chewing on her worry. She halted him as he left the booth. "You don't think—"

He stopped to invent. "The guy who taught me this business advised me not to think. Leave that to the number ones, he used to say. That's the rule I follow." It would give her something else to ponder. It might keep her from confessing her error.

The hot coffee was poured. A cheap brandy stood in liqueur glasses at each of the three places. Janni's glowering anxiety tightened her dark brows. Steve sat down and tasted the brandy before speaking. She'd never ask. It was good to keep her waiting; because he wanted to hurt her and because he couldn't; because he could only strike with these petty twigs.

He said finally to Rube, "I'm sorry I can't give you kids the car. But I'll need it to get to Benedict Canyon. I'll probably be late. Think you can amuse yourself?"

Her violence burst out. She shoved her chair from the table, shouted, "I can amuse myself without your mangy car. I am going to work."

Rube tried to protest but she had no words for him. She lingered only long enough to down the brandy. You learned in the gutters not to waste food or drink. And she was gone, her red coat a streaming danger signal behind her.

Rube was on his feet, not believing this.

Steve said, "Let her go."

"But—"

"She gets that way. Temper."

Rube sat down. Not accepting Steve's dictum. Resenting it. Resenting Steve. He couldn't hold it back for long. "What the hell's the matter with you tonight? There was nothing wrong with Janni until you sat down here and started needling. No wonder she got mad. Every time you opened your mouth, you socked her."

He didn't want to scrap with Rube. And he certainly didn't want, as if he were a spoiled child, to say that she'd started it. Even more he didn't want the soldier getting serious over Janni. He maintained a calm objectivity. Or tried for it. "You forget, I've known that piece a fairly long time. She's not the gay, charming kid she's giving you a picture of. Believe me, she isn't."

"So you can sock her because she's come up from the gutter?"

"Up from the gutter to Skid Row."

Rube's fists knotted.

"Okay," Steve said quickly. "That's not why. I don't care whether she's Skid Row or Bel Air. That has nothing to do with what she is. There's plenty of her kind both places. It's what she's doing to Davidian that burns me up."

"Protecting him?" She'd been at Rube and he'd listened.

"Protecting him? Yeah. From the only guy that can help him, the only friend he's got."

"You?"

"Me."

"You and God and Stalin."

"You're talking like Janni." It wasn't Rube's fault. Janni could take any of them, make pretzels out of them. "Who

124

the hell does she think she is, making Davidian's decisions?"

"If he wants to see you, why doesn't he? He's all over Hollywood, washing dishes, watching Santa Claus." Rube's voice was deadly. "Being careful he's two jumps ahead of you."

Steve downed his coffee. He couldn't give Reuben the whole picture. He was upset about having it like this but there was nothing more he could do or say now. "Sorry. Maybe you're right." He pulled out his wallet, replaced it when Reuben said with austere determination, "This is mine."

And Reuben could be right. Davidian did know that Stefan Winterich was in town; even if Janni had withheld the information, he couldn't help knowing, his ear was against too many of the right keyholes. Steve couldn't be sure of Davidian, you couldn't be sure of any man whose life had been a lie for twenty years. Or more. Davidian might have been born a moral contortionist.

How could a man ever be sure of any other man? This was the age of treachery, the age when the lie was made dogma, when evasion was a sanctified virtue and ignorance a sacrament. It was the age of words but the words no longer had meaning, they had been subverted into the gibberish of the new jungle. There was no more honor; how could Davidian be an honorable man? Loyalty was only a banner to be dragged through the slime; how could Davidian be loyal? In the time of Davidian, there were no verities. No, Steve could trust Davidian no more than he could trust his beloved or his friend. Such trust was archaic, there was no longer a place for such reactionary weakness.

The night was milder than it had been earlier. Steve tossed his coat on the seat beside him and spurred out of the lot. In the small light of the kiosk the slovenly boy continued to pore over his comic book. He didn't look up to find out if the man and the car belonged together.

Steve drove too fast out Sunset to Benedict Canyon. The canyon road lay in darkness and shadow, the road lamps were far apart, the moon and stars too distant for color. The Moritz gate was open and he pulled up to the front of the house. He left his hat with his coat in the car. He touched the discreet white button which caused chimes to sound within the palace. The house was dark save for the faint illumination of the hall. This could be Haig's trap; he would not be surprised. But he'd had to find out.

Feather herself opened the door. When she saw it was he, she said, "Oh, Steve."

The hopes he'd had out of hopelessness that she could deliver the goods, began falling. She couldn't help him if she wanted to, she couldn't even speak a definite hello. But he was here and he went inside. To hear what she had to offer.

She said, "I'm in the library," and she led him towards the far room.

"Did you have any trouble breaking away from your party?"

"No. I said I must go home and rehearse. It's true. I'm auditioning next week for a show." She'd made it true. She'd cleared a space for work and she was wearing ballet slippers. Her hair was tied up with a black cord. It bobbed like a horse's cropped tail.

The French windows were open to the gardens at the back. There'd be a blue pool, under moonlight now; bright striped umbrellas and chaise longues for sun. Janni would have lived in peace and beauty here; this girl somehow seemed cramped in a confine of her own making, afraid to lay her hand on any of the richness. Was a dancer so single-minded? Idly he wondered if she could dance, if perhaps she would come alive in motion and music. He would never find out.

She went to the phonograph and stilled the music. He recognized the bluebird motif from the *Sleeping Beauty.* She gestured to the same low table. "Have a drink?"

"Not now." And he took his same place on the couch, waited for her to press against the same down-cushioned corner. She was fluttery, over being alone with him, over the trap? He said, "You've got something?"

She didn't understand, she curled her hand over to the table where her horn-rimmed glasses were laid.

"On Davidian?"

She said, "Yes." She was more contained with the horn-rims on.

"Well?"

Color flushed into her cheeks as she began. She was stalling for time. "He worked in Berlin, the Eastern zone. Very secret work. No one knows why he wanted to leave or how he managed it." Her hair bobbed nervously. "But he did leave and he's in Los Angeles. Naturally the F.B.I. wants to find him because they hope he'll inform to them about Soviet plans. And the Soviets must find him first because

126

they can't be sure that he won't be made to talk. They can't trust him anyway because of the way he took leave from Berlin." She said anxiously, "No one understands why he's been hiding out from you. You were his friend." She interrupted herself, "You know all this, don't you?"

"Yes," he said. "But I don't know where he is. Did you find out?"

The word broke sharp from the open French windows behind them. "No!"

It wasn't this interruption which Feather was expecting. She turned as quickly, as startled as Steve. Janni was in the room; she came rapidly around the couch to Feather. "You must not tell him. Davidian escaped, he is free. You must not betray him to them."

Feather turned uncertain eyes on Steve.

Janni demanded her attention. "Tell him nothing! He is a Coco."

Bewilderment masked Feather.

Janni cried, "Don't you understand? He is a Communist." She said it plain, cold and plain, "A Communist agent."

Again Feather turned her eyes on Steve. No longer were they uncertain behind the lenses. She came to her feet; she was smaller than Janni because she was without heels, otherwise they would have been equal to each other. At this moment in both, the dark and the fair, was a steely force.

Feather said, "Did you think I didn't know?" And she smiled, a terrible, idiot-proud smile. "I too am a Communist."

Janni was silent. Only her eyes moved, from Feather's pale glistening face to Steve on the couch. Her black bitter eyes admitting her defeat.

Steve covered with a cigarette. He needed a moment for adjustment, while Feather was giving Janni the old pitch about the honor and the glory of the cause. He'd known she was dedicated but he'd thought it was to ballet slippers, not to this work. Feather had been on his side all along, she'd been hanging around Haig Armour for his side, not the reverse.

He let out the smoke slowly as he rose from the couch. His side had placed her on the plane in Kansas City. To watch Haig? Who wasn't even on the case then? Wearily he knew better, it was the same old dog on dog; someone to keep an eye on Steve, an operator so new and so dumb that Steve wouldn't be suspicious of her hanging around him. They'd been right; he hadn't suspected her.

She'd stopped her speech-making and turned to him. "What can we do with her?" He'd never noticed before how small and sharp were her teeth.

He said to Janni, "Get out of here."

Feather sucked in her breath. "No." She clutched his arm, shook it. "You can't let her go. She knows too much."

He set her aside. "Go on," he repeated to Janni.

It was as if she couldn't move, as if the look between them held her frozen. Until Feather thrust forward, pushing a glass to Janni. "Before you go, have a drink."

Steve cut it viciously away from her hand. It fell to the floor but it didn't break. The liquid smeared over the rug like blood.

Feather cried sharply, "Why did you do that?" Her mouth was ugly.

He struck her across the ugliness with such force the back of his hand burned. She stood swaying. Her hair was shaken loose from the cord, it dangled against her cheek. He said, "I'm running this show." He spoke again to Janni. "Get out." Her dark eyes were wide and empty. He shouted it, "I said, get out!"

It shocked her to her senses. She turned and fled to the windows. Without expression he watched her until she was engulfed by the night.

Feather was whimpering in disbelief, "You're letting her go."

He could hear Janni's faint running footsteps. Only when there was no longer sound did he return his attention to Feather. There was a red welt swelling over her mouth. He said to her, "Pick up that glass."

She shivered.

He repeated roughly, "Pick up that glass."

Without looking at him, she bent her knees until she was crouched on the rug. Slowly she picked it up. Her mouth was making little animal sounds. She remained there, crouching, holding it in her hand.

"Put it back on the table."

As slowly she came to her feet. When she had set it down, she stood by the table immobile. He walked over to her and laid his hand on her thin shoulder. It trembled uncontrollably beneath his touch and his anger surged. He spun her about and shoved her towards the couch. She fell back

128

on the cushions, looking up at him. The pupils of her eyes, magnified by her glasses, were distended blackly across the pale irises. The look was of fear but she was excited by her fear.

Later his disgust would rise. For now there was nothing but the anger. "Keep out of my business."

She shook her head, the pale hair slapping vacantly against her cheeks.

He repeated it, making it clear. "Keep out of my business. When I'm on a job, I do it my way. And no punk is allowed to interfere. Didn't they tell you that when they put you on me?"

Her bruised mouth hung half open; her eyes didn't move away from his face.

"I asked you a question."

She had trouble speaking. "He said . . . I'd learn . . . a lot . . ."

"From me? Or about me? I hope you've learned. Just keep out of my way from here on in. I've got a job to do and I don't need you dragging my heels."

She was trying to say something and he waited. She managed to whisper, "You let her go."

As he moved towards the couch she cringed back into the cushions. He kept walking until he was standing above her. "Listen, simple. If you ever do get to where you're running a show, remember this. Don't ever pull an assassination on your own parlor rug. There's nothing harder to get rid of than a body."

He walked out on her with that, still on the hard treads of his anger.

V

HE WENT BY THE path that Janni had taken. No one tried to stop him from leaving. He saw no one as he passed through the quiet gardens, walked around the house and slammed into his car. He got away fast. He was beginning to feel a little sick. If he hadn't been there, Janni would not have escaped. But Feather hadn't had the death cup at hand for Janni; she hadn't expected Janni, only him. Feather hadn't thought that up on her own, she'd been following higher orders. Someone on his side who didn't want him around. Or had become too suspicious.

He'd known it when he struck down the glass, not because he'd been afraid Janni would drink from her enemy's hand, but out of his fury. He'd delayed after only to give Janni a good head start. Let her get away safe. While he handled the trouble. He'd expected trouble but it hadn't materialized out of the twenty-eight other rooms of the Moritz château. That didn't mean it wasn't waiting to catch up with him.

Raising his eyes to his rearview mirror, he caught the shadow there. His voice was a threat. "Come on. Who is it?"

"You are being followed. But carefully."

He knew Janni's accent. He asked, "What are you doing in my car?" He could take any danger alone, but not with her along.

She flared back at him. "I am hitching. How did you expect me to get back to the city?"

"The way you got up the canyon."

"This is the way."

Hidden on the floor in the rear, yes. He'd been careless, he hadn't thought of looking.

"Yes, you are followed."

He too had been watching the mirror. "Yes." The shadow of a lightless car was evident. He was still a couple of turns ahead, no more.

"If you will pull in at the next estate—"

"Don't tell me my business."

She tossed out a laugh. "Who taught you?"

She didn't expect an answer. He said, "Keep your head down. If it's the girl, we're all right. She's a dummy. There could have been others staked out. She was too quick with that drink."

"She was jealous." Again the laugh mocked.

He cut his lights before he swung without warning into the drive, silencing the motor. As he ducked out of vision, he undertoned, "She doesn't give a damn for you or me. She's a fanatic."

He hoped this mansion was far enough from the drive and fast enough in sleep not to investigate a stray car. They were silent as the approaching car neared. It sped by. Steve counted a slow twenty before starting his motor again.

Janni said, "It was the girl. She was alone. Unless someone was hiding with her."

On her way to report failure of the mission. "You took a chance."

"She did not see me," she scorned. "I am experienced."

He let it go, backing without lights.

She told him, "Go in the other direction."

"I know what I'm doing." He was curt but she only laughed again. Nearer now. She was a shadow behind his shoulder. He ordered, "Stay down."

"I am joining you." She was over the seat as light as blown thistle, not touching him in the transition.

"It is better," she said complacently. "She is looking for a man not for a man and his girl." His eyes slanted briefly to her but she was lighting a cigarette. She took one breath of it and passed it into his fingers.

He said, "Thanks." He didn't think about her mouth touching it.

She lit one for herself, pushed into the corner and was quiet. Not until they were beyond homes into the silent darkness of the canyon, did he pull off the road.

She cried out, "Why do you stop?" Her eyes pried into the darkness.

He assured her, "We're safe," and said bluntly, "I want to talk to you."

This time he lit the cigarettes, passed one to her. She shivered a little but he didn't notice. She didn't say thanks.

He didn't know what to say, he'd said it all. He couldn't knock the information he needed out of her. She couldn't be cajoled or threatened or tricked. She was too experienced; she'd been tempered in Berlin for too long and too often. For some reason of her own, she would protect Davidian, even to the extent of walking into danger herself.

The cigarettes made a thin fog between them. She said, "You should not have struck her."

"She needed it." He said, "Don't waste any tears on her. She wanted to kill you."

"I know," she said simply. "But it was dangerous to strike her." She turned in the seat to see his face. "Her uncle is a most important man. To the party."

He hadn't known it. He didn't tell her. He boasted, "So am I."

"He is more important. He is Mr. Moneybags. They need him more than they need you."

She always knew so much more than he. "Who told you?"

"Everyone knows."

"Then what made you come barging out to Feather with your big news about me? Did you think it would surprise her?"

"I could not believe she was one of you," she said. "So stupid. You admit she is stupid."

"Sure. Stupid. And dangerous." He went back to the question. Because he must know. "Who told you about Moritz?"

"It is easy to learn these things. There are some of us who keep our eyes and ears open. Some who have escaped once from the terror and who do not wish to be forced to run again. It is wisdom to keep informed."

Davidian had told her, Davidian, who hung around picking up information in the right spots.

Her eyes glittered in the dark. "When you tell them of me, tell them they will never find all of those who watch them. They may erase me, but I am nothing. They may kill Davidian—but when one of us dies, there are many more who take our place."

"I'm not going to tell them about you."

"Why not?" Contempt sat lightly on her lips. "They will be proud of you that you have discovered a new plot. The watchers and the listeners. Perhaps they will decorate you with two red bloody stars, one for Davidian, one for—"

He put rough hands on her arms. Between his teeth he told her "I'm not trying to kill Davidian. I'm trying to help him. How can I make you believe me?"

He shouldn't have touched her. He shouldn't have been

132

with her here in the isolation of the night, his fingers biting into the flesh beneath her red coat, their eyes locked in hate one for the other. Her lips moved but she said nothing. From him without volition came one word, one desperate cry, "Janni!"

And he was holding her to him, so desperately, so close that they were one shadow. "My darling . . . my darling. . . ." He whispered it, trying to bring her more close to him, his hands under her coat, after this eternity of time warming themselves again on the fire of her body. Blindly he found her mouth. And he held her, so that the fibers of his suit would be imprinted on her flesh, holding in her the deepest wells of the earth and the sharpest ecstasy of the stars. When he drew away it was so little, only that he might look into the wonder of her face.

She smiled up at him. "Stefan." Her hand touched his cheek gently. She was not gentle. "Stefan. I have been alone."

He said, "I love you." He hadn't said the words for so long that they were as a strange language. They were good, the old words, the simple words. They were honest. He was not ashamed to say them over, "I love you, Janni."

"We can be together now." Her voice was rich as the fruits of the earth. "As you promised we would be."

He couldn't lie to her. Not even to quiet his own agony.

She stirred in his arms to see his face. As if she didn't know what would be there. She cried out, "We can be together now? Stefan, Stefan—"

He whispered again, "My darling . . . my darling . . ."

"Stefan." She hid her face against his arm. She wasn't made of weakness, after a moment she raised her head. "Take me with you, Stefan. Wherever you go, take me. I can always get a job. I can sell tickets in cheap movies anywhere in the world. No one will know I am with you. I'll keep out of sight, I will never let them know."

It was the time to bargain. To ask for Davidian in exchange for a promise of their happiness. A promise he couldn't keep. He kissed her and knew the flame of her hope. When he put her away, he again lighted cigarettes for both of them. He said, "If I can get this job ticked off—"

She moved in the curve of his arm.

His eyes held on the dark road ahead. "I'm due a vacation. Maybe we could get a car and just take off. See the country. I'd like to show you the country." He went on just as if she were an innocent who could believe his words. "Texas and New York and Missouri and Cape Cod."

"As once you promised we would." She could make believe too. "And we'll choose the one we like the most and find there a little house—"

"And live on clams or hominy grits or fried chicken—" The dreams a man dreams. He broke off and his voice was like cinders. "Where's Davidian?"

She regarded the glowing tip of her cigarette for a long, long time. She said, "He's waiting for me at the Main Street movie."

He didn't release his breath. He took another pull at his cigarette, it was burned almost to his fingers but he held on to it. He had to hold on to something. "Alone, Janni. I'll have to see him alone. You can't be there."

She didn't say anything. She was crying. Janni didn't cry.

He pitched his cigarette out of the window, took hers from her mouth and threw it away. "Janni—" She came to him but there was no longer hope in her, only the same desperation of passion that had eaten away his heart. He memorized her with his hands and his mouth as if he would never again be permitted to touch her. "Janni. Tomorrow—"

She cried, "Tonight! Take me home with you."

"I can't." It was the final bitterness. "I couldn't anyway. Reuben—"

She was defeated. "And I am not alone. The old ones are always there."

"Tomorrow night. I'll fix it up some way, baby. I'll be through the job. I'll come for you early, you can say your aunt is sick—"

She put her hand across her eyes. But she wasn't crying any longer. "You'll come, Stefan?"

He said from his deepest heart, "I promise you. There isn't anyone or anything that will keep me away tomorrow night." He'd make sure of it. He'd lay the plans so carefully that nothing could take away this one night for them. They deserved one small scrap of life.

She lifted her head. "Take me downtown now, Stefan. I'm late but Joe understands. He believes Reuben is my sweetheart, leaving for overseas duty. Tomorrow night I will wait for you."

"I'll come," he repeated quietly.

There were no other cars that followed the lonely road to Mulholland, dropped down again into the city. He drove in silence; she remained apart, she might be sleeping but

134

she wasn't asleep. When they reached Spring Street, she said, "Don't drive to the theater. It's better I go alone."

"Yes." He pulled up to the curb.

She looked into his eyes. But all she said was, "Davidian will be safe?"

"I promise you."

"Give me time to get there. Do not know me when you buy a ticket. You will find him inside. He always sits on the left. He does not sleep, he likes movies."

She was gone with no more words. He idled the motor until she had turned the corner on Main. He waited a little longer before following. Main Street was tinny-bright. Loud-speakers squalled music from open doors; there were boys in sailor suits and soldier suits just as if it were war days, girls in paintbox dresses edging in on them. Honky-tonk bars were open-armed. Laughter was hysterical. He drove past the gaudy nightmare, past pawnshop row, past her theater and into the block of the missions. He turned on Second at the dark Cathedral corner. At the end of the block he found a space, parked and locked the car. You didn't take chances in a neighborhood like this one.

She was enclosed in the glass booth. Even the old bums who bought tickets would know she was beautiful; they wouldn't know why she was more beautiful tonight. She had a magazine on her knees, it was open but she wasn't reading it, not tonight. She glanced up when his shadow fell on her.

His bones ached to splinter the glass, to consign to hell the Davidian report, the oaths and the loyalties, the dangers and the rewards. There was nothing that mattered, nothing but his need for her. He said, "One," and put down his coin. Her hand didn't touch the ticket, a machine shoved it at him. Her eyes went down to her magazine at once, there was no betrayal but the quick rise and fall of the silk covering her breasts.

The punk at the door didn't know him. He accepted the stub and let Steve pass into the ill-smelling box. There was no usher. Steve stood at the rear until his eyes could adjust to the dark. The screen was noisy, mounted cowboys were clattering bullets into a mountain pass. When he could distinguish the seats, he started slowly down the left aisle. The theater wasn't half full; it was early, not yet midnight. There were some kids clustered together but the derelicts sat apart from each other, suspicious of their own kind. He recognized the shape of a head, or hoped he did, halfway

135

down the left aisle, the aisle seat left vacant for a friend. No one close enough to overhear a word spoken under the tongue. Steve slid into the empty seat. He didn't turn his head to make sure.

"It took you long enough to come," the mutter insinuated.

"I have a car."

"Where is it?"

"East of Main on Second. End of the block." He was ready to lift out of his seat.

But Davidian murmured, "I must see the end of the picture. The end is very exciting. He rides the villain over the edge of the parapet."

"You've seen it once?"

"I have seen it since nine o'clock." The titter was soundless.

"For Christ's sake."

"It is very exciting."

The house lights didn't come up at the finish. This was a bedchamber for men who hadn't the price of a bed.

"You go first. I follow."

Steve obeyed. Not certain Davidian would show up. Even now he didn't trust Davidian. Especially now, because being with the man was to be reminded of the silverfish elusiveness. He couldn't be certain Davidian wouldn't stay for the third or fourth showing. Very exciting.

Steve didn't look at Janni as he left the theater. It was better not to see her. He was unlocking the car door when Davidian materialized beneath his shoulder. Steve hadn't heard him approach.

"Not much of a car," Davidian commented.

"It beats walking."

"You are too easily satisfied. Give me a cigarette. I have just run out."

"Did you ever buy a pack?"

Davidian chuckled agreeably. "Thank you." He took four, deliberately, tucked them into his shirt pocket. A fifth he put between his lips. "A match, if you please."

Steve handed him a used folder.

"It is like old times, Stefan," Davidian mused.

"You've missed me?" He asked it, "You have the report finished?"

"Did I not promise you?"

It was going to be all right, he could relax. "Where do we go?"

"We do not go together, Stefan. Have you forgotten so
136

soon what you have learned? Or do you believe there is no danger in Hollywood?"

"I'm not quite the fool you've been."

Davidian offered his amused cough. "You have been hearing of me?"

"Why do you take such chances?"

"Stefan, Stefan," Davidian choked. "There was no risk. Davidian knew what he was doing." Always he'd had the colossal conceit of the great of the earth, this half-starved puny man in the broken shoes, the shabby coat, the bare head with its thin covering of hair. "The chance I do not take is to drive to my house with Stefan Winterich. This risk is too great."

"You mean I'm poison?"

Davidian puffed on the cigarette. "You do not know?"

"Maybe I do," Steve said savagely. "Well, how do we do it?"

Davidian considered. Quite as if he hadn't thought it out carefully in advance. "You will let me out." He considered it more thoughtfully. "It is Saturday night, yes. At the Palladium, a palace of the dance on Sunset Boulevard near Gower, I will leave the car. I will mingle with the departing dancers and those leaving the broadcast studios."

"We meet where?"

Davidian whispered the street. "The brown house. Once it was a brown house. A modest house. To suit a modest man."

"Who gets there first?"

"It matters not." He'd smoked the cigarette to its burning ash. He flipped it regretfully out of the window. "You will have the key." He palmed it from his pocket, a ten-cent key, the kind that opened a dozen doors. "If I am not there yet, you will visit with Stella. I leave it to you what you tell her. One thing only, no one must see you come." He wasn't mocking now.

"You think I'm still walking around because I take chances?"

"No, Stefan. You do not take chances. You are a careful man." There was only the faintest flavor of contempt.

"Who's Stella?"

"A very fine woman. She tries to fatten me. For her sake, I venture to believe." He sighed noisily. "Poor Stella. I am unworthy of her."

"Is she safe?"

137

"But Stefan, how can you ask? She knows nothing! When I leave she knows no more."

Steve understood. "That's how you've hidden. Kept moving."

"An Arab in the night."

"Yes. Without folding your tent." Before neighbors could grow too neighborly. Before they became curious.

Davidian wheezed, "How can one, when there is no tent to fold?"

The sky lights of Hollywood were moving closer to the windshield. Davidian said, "You will drive a little more carefully and the red light will stop you at Gower."

Davidian had the car door open before the wheels were motionless. Steve didn't turn his head. There might have been no one beside him in the car. Fleetingly he wondered if he would catch up with Davidian again.

2

When the light changed, Steve drove on to Vine, followed it to Hollywood Boulevard and headed west. He was uneasy passing Davidian's street. It was an empty street, only two houses on it, an unused street, the business offices shuttered, not even the inevitable Hollywood parking lot to give it light and movement. There was no reason for anyone to walk into the mouth of that street at night except to visit one of the two houses. And he had to go there unseen. Again he cursed Davidian, it must have been deliberate; only someone seeking to make danger would have insinuated himself into one of those houses.

He drove on up the boulevard to Highland, followed it to an all-night filling station. He left the car for gas while he went into the office and rang Oriole. The anxious voice said, "Where have you been? I have tried to reach you."

Steve snapped, "Where do you think I've been? Working. I'm coming around. In about thirty minutes. It's important."

"You have found—?" There was hope.

"I've got plenty to report. Thirty minutes." He hung up. With Steve expected in thirty minutes, none of them would be currycombing the streets for him.

He paid the attendant and drove on. Mr. Oriole would be getting Mr. Schmidt out of bed. Unless they were all there now, the careful Schmidt, an hysterical Feather, and a rich irate uncle. They'd forgive if he brought them the Davidian report. He wondered if Elsabeth was in it too. But certainly, her diamonds would have an extra glitter because of the secrets she shared of a great day coming, secrets her lunch and tea and cocktail ladies didn't dream. Aunt Elsabeth would think her diamonds were to be safe.

He circled in and around before parking the car on Franklin, north of the boulevard. Not too far from his destination, but far enough so that if anyone should spot the heap, they'd have a hard time knowing which way he had headed.

He walked unhurriedly to Davidian's. At the mouth of the street he cut the corner boldly. Davidian might not be so foolish after all. You could be sure if you were alone here. He faded into the alley before approaching the houses, noting the courtyard behind them, the back door of the once-brown house, the flat roof obtruding from the second story, an easy drop into the yard. He waited, listening, but no footsteps crept after him. He was swift moving to the house; he opened the door with Davidian's key and closed it fast.

He was in a narrow unlighted hallway. He stood there not moving, his hand on the doorknob behind him, unsure as he must be always with the slippery Davidian. Wondering if the enemy had offered better terms, if this were the ultimate trap. And then there was a scratch on sand and a firefly glimmer of light. He looked up to it, saw the shape of Davidian at the head of the stairway. The glimmer disappeared and Steve climbed the stairs in its memory, followed the darker shadow in the dark another flight. The stairs ended at a door, a door which opened on well-oiled hinges. When it was closed, Davidian struck another match.

"The attic room," he said sardonically. With the match spurt he found a low lamp, turned it on. No light could show to the street below. The windows were curtained in black.

The ceiling was low, the walls bare, the floor unpainted. There was a broken cot; an upholstered chair, its cotton molting from the arms and side; a crippled dining table and discarded chairs. Davidian was a collector. There were orange crates, corrugated boxes, the quite good lamp. Steve sat on one of the chairs.

"You like it, Stefan?" Davidian showed his discolored teeth. "I knew you would feel at home here." He rooted into a box and brought forth a bottle of red wine. "This too for your homesickness." From an orange crate he took two unmatched glasses. "I am sorry there is no woman, but a man is not permitted everything." He overfilled the tumblers, bent and sipped from the best one. "Not bad, this

139

California vintage. I am becoming a good American even to my palate."

"Besides it's easier to find a bottle on an unguarded shelf."

There had been no other way to keep alive in the world of Davidian. It was not dishonesty, it was survival. When all else had been stripped from man, one law alone remained, to survive.

Davidian said cheerfully, "You are insulting." He settled in the musty armchair, as if it were a throne. "Ah, it is like old times, Stefan." He reached for his glass. "A cigarette, if you please."

"There are four in your pocket," Steve reminded him.

Davidian refrained from smoking. Biding his time until absent-mindedly he could reach for one when Steve brought out his pack. As he knew Steve would. And as Steve knew, it was an old gamble between them. Like old times but no rustle of Janni behind the door, cutting the bread and cheese, her happy heart singing an accompaniment to the men's words. Tonight the pain of her had eased, for separation was temporary; there must be a means whereby they could run away together tomorrow night, if only for brief respite. He had the car, a few hours and they could be over the border into Mexico. They could be married in Mexico. He was turning soft thinking marriage, that came from a trip home, away from the ugly realities of Berlin.

Yet, sipping the sweet wine—Davidian's taste was appalling—he did not outthrust the idea with violence as he had in the past, knowing it to be treachery to Janni to take her as wife. He was growing too old for the life he had chosen at the finish of the second war for power. He could be valuable at a desk; the sands of his luck had run out so often, it was time to stop while there was yet time. The end for an agent was always the same unless he could stop, refuse the one more job. With a wife and children, they'd have to let him quit.

Davidian's room was not the place for solemn decision, not with those sly, lizard eyes probing the shadows of your face. He was here on a job. But he was loath to get to it, because with the job done there would be no reason to delay longer with wine and a cigarette and an old, if not trusted, friend. He took out his cigarettes, almost a fresh pack, put one between his lips and absently set the pack in the center of the table. Perhaps favoring himself the slightest bit. Let Davidian reach.

140

He could enjoy a little more time. He had protected himself for at least an hour. "How long did it take you to find this place? How long did you watch it, day after day, for a vacancy, becoming more and more avid for its danger?"

Davidian smiled. "You make it tedious. It was not this way. First there was Stella. I became acquainted with Stella."

"Yes, that way." Steve sighed into the wine. One way or the other with Davidian. A trick or a woman. And he enjoyed success with women somehow, this verminous, feline rodent. Steve asked, "Why did you insist on Hollywood? Was it because Janni had come here?"

Davidian choked. "Stefan, Stefan. Must it always be Janni for you? Are there no other women?"

"Was it?" Steve demanded.

"Yes." He stopped coughing. It was the first honest word he'd spoken. "What man would not choose Hollywood when he had been forced to listen to you and Janni describe it in the rich colors of a Gauguin? You remember? When you were endeavoring to convince Janni she must leave you? Before the danger should become the fact of her being shot by one side or the other because she is generous and sells to both?" Davidian cleared his throat delicately. "She was a stubborn girl. It was difficult for me to convince her that it was you who planned to inform on her." He drank wine. "As you paid me to do. Because you are soft about Janni, because you wish her to be safe." He argued, "Where else would I choose to come when you endeavor to convince me—"

Steve interrupted, "It was because of Janni."

The true Davidian emerged briefly again. The cold dangerous man who dwelt beneath the cap and bells. "Yes, because of Janni. Because you would no longer be around—" He shrank from Steve's face. Then he said simply, "Because only Janni I can trust."

And this could be true. Steve said, "You were not to communicate."

Davidian observed his dirty nails. "But I communicated with Janni."

"Who are the old ones?"

"I found them for Janni. For her protection." The teeth flashed. "She is so desirable, is Janni—" He helped himself openly to a cigarette.

"You didn't trust her too far. She couldn't reach you. You moved too often and without advance notice." She'd told

141

him the truth. "You trusted her only for your own convenience. An address."

"For her cut she is happy to play postmaster."

Steve glowered.

"But certainly. For money she is always happy. Ten per cent." He flung his hands petulantly. "You send me so little."

"It was the best I could do."

"And of this I must pay ten per cent to Janni. After your fine promises, behold me! The attic! The shoes!" He extended them.

"You'll get it all now."

Davidian was eager. "The house? The little car? Money?"

"All of it."

"And my papers. A citizen."

"That takes more time. But you'll get it. In exchange for the report."

Davidian's eyes lidded. "There is something I do not comprehend, Stefan."

"Yes?" Now came trouble.

"The report. Why is it I must run in two directions? Neither the F.B.I. nor the C.P. must know of the report. Why must it be given privately to Stefan Winterich?"

Steve said coldly, "I like a cut myself."

Davidian flicked up greedy eyes.

Steve laughed in his face. "If you think you can make a better deal alone, go on, make it. Would you like to know, my friend, what will happen if you try? The F.B.I. will take your report and dump you back to Berlin. Or the C.P. will take your report and exterminate you, to make sure you do not write another one. In either case—" He cut his forefinger across his throat.

"I am satisfied," Davidian said quickly. "You will give me all you promised?"

"Have I ever lied to you?"

"No. Oh no," Davidian assured him. He drained his glass. Moisture stood on his lip. He eyed the empty bottle. "We need a little more, I think. If you could spare a dollar, Stella may be awake—"

Steve rooted in his pocket, counted a dollar in change. Davidian's fingers closed over the silver. He started to the door, shook his head thoughtfully and returned to the orange crate. "Ah yes! A bottle escaped my eye." The silver jangled in his pocket.

While Davidian's fingers twined around the cork, Steve

142

said, "You knew I was in town. Janni told you. And you saw me at the parade."

The lips tittered. "Yes."

"Why did you keep me waiting?"

Davidian drew the cork with dignity. "You insisted you would come to me when it was safe. I wished it to be safe." He poured for himself alone.

Steve took the bottle from him. "You're a God-damned liar." But he knew why. The man's malice wasn't a trifling thing. Only by making fools of those on top of him had Davidian managed to cling to a shred of dignity. "You do have the report?"

Davidian squirmed into his easy chair. "Must I repeat myself?" His ink-stained fingers warmed themselves on the tumbler. "Not so much a liar, my dear Stefan. It will surprise me if you complete this job in good health." He toasted Steve silently. "I am your friend. I tell you this because I am your friend. I planned to welcome you when you arrived but the plane was too late."

"Albion?"

"Is dead," Davidian said complacently. "You believed he was your friend. You did not know he had become suspicious. Too suspicious. Poor Albion."

Steve shook his clanging head.

"Did you believe he visited the F.B.I. as an informer? Did you not know he was looking for information about you?" He repeated, "Poor Albion, he wished so badly to lay his hands on the report. How surprised he was the night I permitted him to catch up with me! And how happy. Because now he could get the report for his good friend Stefan. For no other reason, to be sure, but to surprise you at the airport by having it in his hands. He was even willing that I too should meet you at the airport, when I was reluctant to permit him to carry the papers." The lips drew back over the pointed teeth. "So trusting, our good friend Albion. He believed I too was trusting."

"If I'd been on time—"

"How simple it would have been. None of this hocus-pocus. Albion and you and I. Old friends meeting. He did not know he would become sleepy. You were too late. I could not remain after Albion—"

Steve said huskily, "Skip it."

"We are friends?"

"Yes." He'd have done it himself, have been forced to do it to eliminate the threat. There were no friends; there was

143

only the imperative: Survive! The wine was making Steve sick. "Where's the report?"

"You have a purchaser?"

"I've told you often enough, yes. Hand it over."

"I am a careful man." Davidian sighed. "But who knows when I am not careful enough? It would not be safe here where I live with my wine and my books."

Steve spat the words. "Where is it?"

"It is safe." He mouthed slyly, "Tomorrow—"

Steve was out of the chair. "Why waste my time tonight?"

"It is a waste of time to drink wine and talk of the old days with a friend?"

Steve spoke one cold warning. "I can't sell it until I get my hands on it."

"I will bring it to you tomorrow." He smiled piously. "Not too early. First I must play the organ at Dr. Ormigon's church. You did not know I am a musician?"

Hidden in the organ. Or under the altarpiece. Or in the preacher's Bible. Yes, the report was safe.

"How will you get it to me?"

Davidian patronized. "That will be my problem. Yours will be to arrange the quick sale. You notice I trust you, I ask for no receipt." No receipt; only a knife in the guts, a noose for a collar, Albion wine for betrayal. "You will be careful leaving here. It is well you carry something, just in case." He went to his dirty cot, lifted the mattress. "My books. You did not know I am a poet?" He selected a small volume. The binding was of rotting leather, the pages were pen-written with cramped letters. "You will not be able to read these, I regret, they are in Rumanian." He put it in Steve's hands. "It is well to carry a bone to toss to the wolves."

"It's safe to toss this?"

"Perfectly safe. It is not my best poetry." The lips twisted. "But should you be discovered leaving, you have been visiting Stella. She will agree."

Steve nodded. He slipped the volume into his jacket pocket. His topcoat would cover the additional bulk.

Davidian said suddenly, "Be careful the popcorn man does not see you depart. I do not wish to leave Stella yet." His smile was mocking. "He watches this house often, a suspicious man, but I am too clever for him." He hesitated, and then continued, "He and Albion were good friends. Possibly Albion confided in him? I would not wish any harm to

144

come to you until after the sale is complete, you understand."

Davidian held open the door until Steve had descended to the sleeping second floor. From there on Steve walked in darkness. It was safer in the dark. He did not need to go outside to spot the little yellow lantern. It was reflected in the window glass of the front door.

He retreated to the rear of the house. He knew the password should he be challenged: Stella. He slid the bolt on the kitchen door and was outside. A silent bolt, a silent door; Davidian was a handy man about the house. Steve was as silent on the kitchen's shallow steps. Protecting himself against the wall of the house, he edged to the corner, to where he could glimpse the street. The popcorn cart blocked the mouth of the alley. Again he retreated, brushing the wall, until he reached the back steps. There was no way out except across the empty courtyard. The house masked it from the street but when he ducked out into the shadows at the far end of the alley, he was observed. He heard the piping little whistle and the rattle of wheels. Without appearing to pick up speed, he lengthened his stride.

Hollywood had gone to bed, the streets were deserted as those of a lost city. The cops were never around when you needed them. He didn't want cops, he must go it alone. It was no more than a half-block to Hollywood Boulevard but he stuck to the alleyways. He'd have a chance to elude the popcorn man in their murk, none at all on the lighted boulevard. At this hour it, too, was a desolate road.

The bobbing yellow lantern, the faint whistle followed inexorably. Steve didn't run, only a frightened man took to his heels. He wasn't afraid but he couldn't afford to answer questions tonight. Because he wasn't hampered by a pushcart, he was able to outstrip the popcorn man. He cut over to the boulevard just below his hotel. And knew he'd been tricked, the yellow lantern waited on the corner. There was no way out of it but to brass. He walked steadily to the danger.

The man beside the cart wasn't anyone, he was motley, he'd fade into a crowd. Unless you'd had experience you wouldn't recognize in his face the marks of the beast. He said, just passing the time, "Out kinda late, Mister. Popcorn?" His voice was scratchy, as if phlegm were lodged in his throat.

Steve shook his head and kept on walking.

"I been waiting for you."

He stopped. "What for?"

"You been wanting to see me."

"I don't now."

"You stayed pretty long in the brown house."

"Yeah?"

"I missed you when you come out." He took hold of the handles of the cart, preparatory to turning it. "Guess you got plenty to say to Mr. Oriole."

Steve said quietly, "I'm not going to Oriole's."

"They been waiting a long time."

"Tough."

"They sent me to fetch you. I kinda guessed you might be at Stella's house." The grimace wasn't pretty.

Steve demanded, "Do you know who I am?"

"Stefan Winterich." It didn't mean a thing to him, a man Oriole wanted fetched, no more.

"Go back to Oriole's," Steve said. "Ask the boss, the big boss, to let you have a look at the directions on Stefan Winterich's job."

Uncertainty began to trouble the man's face.

"Ask him for the Berlin directive. If you can read, take a look at the signature." He smiled at the sudden fear glazing the porcine eyes. "And present my compliments to Mr. Oriole and his guests. Tell them I miscalculated slightly. I'll meet them tomorrow night instead, early, say ten o'clock." The business wouldn't take long once it was set up. Janni went on the Main Street job at ten; he'd pick her up within an hour of that.

Steve's tongue whipped. "If anyone doesn't like it, tell him to read that directive." He walked away then, across the street to his hotel.

The old man with the dyed hair was behind the desk. Steve said, "Don't put any calls through until noon. Just in case you forget, I'm leaving the phone off the hook."

The lights were on in his room, Reuben's bags were packed, the kid was lying on the bed in full uniform. He was wide awake. "I thought you'd never get here." His smile was hesitant.

Steve said, "You're not leaving?" He'd almost forgotten the words between them, it seemed months ago.

"I have to be in San Francisco tomorrow. My orders were waiting for me when I got back to the hotel. I'd been expecting them."

"You can't leave at this hour." Steve flung his hat and coat at the chair.

"I figured on getting out at midnight." The smile flickered. "But I couldn't walk out without seeing you, not after—" He talked fast, embarrassed. "My old man always said two guys can't carry one dame. It just doesn't work. I'm sorry, Steve."

Steve tried not to sound too tired. "Don't apologize. I should have kept my mouth shut."

"I've been trying to call Janni. To say good-by."

"She's all right," Steve told him. "I found her."

Reuben must have been able to see it was all right. He said, "You'll tell her I tried."

"I sure will."

He chewed the end of a match. "She thinks a lot of you, Steve. She's afraid of this business you're mixed up in."

Steve lay on his bed. The book was a stone slab in his pocket. "Did she tell you about Berlin?"

Rube didn't answer. He wondered how much she had told the boy. Of a guy who deserted the American Army after beating up a snivel-nosed major who accused him of operating on the black market? Of a guy who joined up with the Cocos in the Eastern zone? Or only of love in the rubble.

Steve said, "She needn't worry. I know what I'm doing. Didn't she tell you I was the smartest operator in the business?"

Rube's face was torn apart. He was very young.

Steve said, "I thought you were here on a job. To watch me. I still don't know." And because he didn't know, he had to force things, instead of shaking hands and saying, *I'll see you kid.* "What was your job in Berlin? Why were you sent home just when I was?"

Reuben said dully, "My outfit's being transferred to the Pacific. We got a week's furlough. There wasn't any reason to hang around New York. My old lady's shacked up with a new boy friend. I told you that. My old man's too busy for me. All the other guys went home. I wanted to have a little fun." He didn't look at Steve. "I don't know what you're trying to tell me. I don't want to know. I'm nothing but a private, first class. If I thought you were—" He looked at Steve then, out of salty blue eyes. "You've been swell to me. You didn't have to take me on. I don't want to know about your job. Janni's still in love with you."

Steve let out his breath slowly. "Whatever anybody tells you, Reuben, this is God's truth. I'm here only for one rea-

147

son, to take care of a friend of mine. Davidian." In a way it was God's truth.

"That's good enough for me." It wasn't but the boy wouldn't start brooding again until he was alone. He wondered if Steve had found Davidian but he didn't ask. It was better not to ask questions.

Steve said, "You'd better get some sleep. You'll be falling over your own feet before you get to San Francisco. The bus is hell."

"The bus is out," Rube said. "I'll have to fly now to make it." He stretched out on the bed again. "I'll catch another nap. I had one while I was waiting for you. Until your laundry came."

Steve raised up cautiously. "My laundry?"

"In the chair." A flat brown-paper parcel. "A shirt they forgot. The guy said he thought you might be needing it for Sunday."

Steve was steady-voiced. "Who brought it? When?"

"Just before you got in. A hell of a time to be delivering the laundry." Reuben laughed. "I think the little guy had been out on the town. With a bottle of vino."

Two bottles. Steve opened the bundle just as if it weren't important. As if it contained only a shirt. That was what it was, a shirt. A silk shirt, the white yellowed by time, not a very clean shirt. Covered every inch with what appeared to be a scroll pattern in black, but was infinitely small letters inscribed by an engraver's fine hand.

Safe delivery. It wasn't often that Steve loved his fellow man but for this single moment he loved Davidian. Steve, not the book of poems, was the bone flung to delay the wolves while Davidian completed safe delivery. It would be the devil's own job to unravel the letters, possibly coded, probably in the little man's own Rumanian tongue. There were trained men for such work. It wasn't Steve's worry.

And how else could Davidian have protected the report but by wearing it on his back when he fled from cave to cave? Where else was it safer than in a nest of dirty laundry when Davidian was trotting about the streets of Hollywood playing his little jokes?

Steve crumpled the paper and string into the waste basket. He opened his suitcase to put this shirt in with his clean ones, and felt something in the pocket. He drew out a fresh-minted ruble. He began to laugh, he couldn't help it. The mark of authenticity, Davidian's calling card.

Reuben said, "Something's funny?"

Steve shook his head. "Delivering laundry at two A. M.!
I was wondering what his boss would say!"

Reuben laughed with him. In his attic Davidian would
be coughing until he choked with mirth.

3

You couldn't tell time by the windows. But his watch
read four when Steve rolled off the bed. Reuben was quick.
"You can't sleep either?"

"No use wasting any more time. I'm going to shower and
change."

Rube put on the light. "I never can sleep when I'm hungry.
Wonder if there's an all-night stand hereabouts."

Steve was stripping off his clothes. "I could do with a
cup of coffee myself." He stopped midway to the bathroom.
"Look, Rube, you want to do something for me?"

There was scarcely a hesitation. "Sure, Steve."

"I had to leave the car last night. If you'd pick it up."
He dug out the key. "It's on Franklin, around Wilcox. If
you'll bring it around, I can run you out to the airport."

"You don't need to—" Rube began.

Steve's slow smile stopped the protest. "You're doing me
the favor, kid. I'll even throw in a big breakfast." He locked
the door after Rube. He didn't waste any time in the shower;
he was dressed again when the soldier returned.

Rube said, "I parked it by the side door. Plenty of room
this time of the day." He took up his khaki bag.

Steve buttoned his topcoat over the book. They stopped
at the desk. Steve said, "I'm not checking out. Just the
soldier." He left the room key. Nothing upstairs for anyone
to find.

He didn't care particularly if anyone followed, taking
Rube to the airport was legitimate. He could get clear later.
But there weren't any signs of activity. No one got up this
early in Hollywood.

The morning turned a pale gray as the car traveled
through the sleeping streets. Steve swung over to Olympic
at Fairfax. "We ought to find a place to eat somewhere
along the way. Don't know that the airport café would be
open at this hour. You're not in a rush, are you?"

"If you're not, I'm not. I'll probably have to wait around
for a seat on a flight."

Rube picked the place. It looked good and they were far
enough from Hollywood not to worry about being inter-

rupted. If they'd been going to run into interference it would have developed now, or it would wait until after he'd dropped the soldier.

They sat at the counter, ordered big—orange juice, oatmeal, ham and eggs, stack of wheats, coffee. Steve knew he couldn't touch half of it, not at this hour and with his stomach nerves like guitarstrings. But Rube could eat double. It was his good-by party.

There was a phone box hung on the wall the same as at Oriole's. He didn't have to have a booth. "I'm going to make a call." He could dial the exchange he needed from this location. He held on while the line rang. The counterman was busy at the grill. Rube was watching the sizzle of the ham.

The voice came on the other end. "Hello."

"Hello. Mack in?" It didn't matter what he said. As long as the other party made the right answers.

"What number do you want?"

His mouth bit into the mouthpiece. "W-5." He drew back, "Yeah, I'll hold on."

The answers were right now. He was memorizing instructions. "Okay, I'll call later."

He returned to the counter. Reuben asked no questions. He was eating. The counterman was reading the Sunday funnies.

Continuing on west they passed early churchgoers. At this hour there was no heavy traffic on Sepulveda, they were at the airport too soon. Steve didn't waste a quarter on the robber barons who guarded the endless acres fenced in for parking. He drew the car to the curb in front of the terminal.

Reuben said, "Thanks for everything, Steve." His handclasp was warm and strong. But things weren't the same. "Good luck."

"Thanks, kid." He wanted to say a lot more. But all he said was, "Maybe we'll run into each other again someday. If the big shots can ever figure out that peace can pay bigger than war."

Rube grinned. "I hope we don't have to wait that long." From the curb, he said, "Tell Janni good-by."

The tall thin uniform, young and crumpled, walked away to the terminal. Steve drove off. Death in a ditch, death in a gutter, what difference? The fruits of war. Maybe Rube was a lucky one, maybe he'd come back with medals and the same easy grin, maybe he'd have a little house someday like any little house and a nice girl and a couple of kids. He could dream for Rube too.

Before heading over to the beach road, Steve took his gun from his pocket and locked it in the glove compartment. He didn't want its weight on him all day. He made sure that there was no one following him on the beach road north. At this hour you could tell. The surf was tossing restlessly, the water was dull as the sky. He parked where he'd been told, above the canyon on the road to Malibu. He slid down the shallow incline to a strip of sand. The sun was watery, the air had not warmed up yet. But he stripped to the waist, made a pile of his clothes, lay on the sand. If there were California nuts who sunned without sun, he was okay. He was following orders.

He wasn't there long before the surf fisherman showed up. The fisherman wasn't cold; he was padded in a sheepskin jacket and heavy whipcords, a peaked cap and wading boots. Steve waited a little longer before he spoke up. "Any luck?"

The fisherman turned his face, it was round and bland, his eyeglasses were rounder. His shaggy white eyebrows joggled. "Not yet." He dropped his worn basket into the sand beside Steve. "You like fishing, son?"

"Haven't the patience. Is there a lookout?"

"Yes. Have to get up early to be a good fisherman." He babbled on like some Izaak Walton.

Neither man was conscious of the basket while Steve transferred the folded yellow shirt covered with its minute scrollwork. "There's a book too which might be useful. Might not." Another sleight of hand and it lay on the shirt. "He called it something to toss to the wolves. You can't trust him."

"Never could."

"You can pick him up at Dr. Ormigon's church this morning. He plays the organ for services. Maybe."

"Maybe not." The fisherman took off his cap to protect his pipe from the offshore breeze. He was bald as a seal.

"I'll be at Oriole's tonight at ten."

"Rather early."

"I've got a date after," Steve grinned. "I'll have friends there."

"Don't worry about that." The old fellow had got the pipe glowing. It looked like a stove.

Steve began to button on his shirt. He was goose-pimples. "Think maybe I could manage a little vacation?"

151

"I can't answer that one."

"Where's the report for me?"

"You'll find it on the floor of your car. Take good care of it today."

"Don't worry." Steve was standing now, buttoning his coat to the chin. A quart of hot coffee might thaw him. And a quart of brandy.

"You'd be smart to get lost today."

"Yeah." He pulled his hat over his forehead. "He killed Albion. He says."

"Albion caught up with him?"

"He says with both of us."

"He's always been a liar. But it could be. Albion was clever."

"Yes." He waved a hand. "Good fishing, Pop."

"Takes patience." He cast his line into the surf.

The car was where he'd left it. Undisturbed. On the floor was the other report. He heeled it under the seat with the sludge and crumbs and chewing-gum wrappers. No one would look for it there. There wasn't any sign of a lookout, just cars from the south driving towards the north, cars from the north driving to the south. The sun was clear, it was going to turn into a blue day. A day to take your girl to the beach, later on build a fire of driftwood, later still watch the stars come out, one times a million stars. Tomorrow. He and Janni would follow the coast of Baja tomorrow. It would be warmer and bluer and there'd be a million times a million stars to cover them.

Get lost. Pull into a motel, get some of that lost sleep before nightfall. Pass time easy. Keep away from Haig Armour. Run like hell from Schmidt's boys.

He couldn't take it easy. Not until he'd seen Haig. He drove back into Beverly Hills, up the bowered driveway of the swank hotel, parked the old crate. It looked worse than ever among the Cadillacs and palm trees.

He asked at the discreet desk for Haig Armour. The clerk couldn't have been more courteous had Steve belonged knee-deep in carpet. He checked and then recalled cheerfully that Mr. Armour was at the pool.

It was warm around the pool. There were some pretty, bronze starlets sunning in beach chairs, some dark and virile athletes showing off on the high board. The rhythmic thud of a tennis ball on the adjoining courts was counterpoint to the splash of the shining water. Haig was resplendent in bathing trunks. He left the cluster of sun bathers when he saw Steve. "Were you looking for me?"

"Surprised?"

Haig drew a bright canvas chair up to one of the white-painted tables. He gestured Steve to another. "I am rather," he admitted.

The sun was too hot in this protected area. "Why? Feather turn me in?" Steve shed his topcoat. "But you know more about me than she could tell you."

"She says you attacked her."

"Does she? You know more about her than I ever will." Steve put his fist on the table. "Maybe she'll move over to your side now. That's all these kids are looking for, something to believe in, something to work for, and a little excitement thrown in. Why can't you get them on your side?"

"Feather's not the ordinary kid."

"No, not exactly. Maybe she isn't worth worrying about. But most of them are."

Haig said tiredly, "We try. Maybe not hard enough." A white-coated boy shadowed the table. Haig asked, "Too early for a drink?"

"Not a beer."

"Two." He waited until the shadow faded. He was casual. "I heard you'd blown town."

"Without the report?" Steve smiled. "Reuben left. I told the hotel I'd be back. Your spies must be suspicious bastards."

"They lost you after you left the airport. Have you found Davidian?"

Strange how you could be having the chills one hour, sweating it out the next. The beer was just right. "I'm still looking." He asked it. "What was Albie after at F.B.I. headquarters?"

Haig said, "You don't know?"

"I don't."

Haig studied him. "He might have been trying to make a deal. He might have been using that as a false face to find out if you'd make a deal. Who killed him?"

"I did. Radar." It was hard to say what he'd come to say. "One thing I want you to know. Janni's an innocent bystander."

Haig didn't say anything.

"That's all she's been in this whole business. She's not mixed up in it in any way."

153

Haig went on listening.

"Just because we knew each other a long time ago, don't get the idea she's on my side. She's here clean. She wants to be a good American. That may sound corny to you, but that's all she wants. She's working for that."

"It may sound corny to you," Haig said. "Not to me."

"Give her a chance. Leave her alone."

"Maybe I can help her."

Steve stilled the brutal pound of his heart. Sure, Haig could help her. She'd be valuable to Haig's outfit, she knew the ropes. Haig could help her in too many ways. You couldn't call a man a bastard when you were asking a favor. If tonight brought the ultimate danger, Janni would have someone to look out for her. Nothing was going to happen, not on an easy job like this.

"I just wanted you to know," Steve said.

He walked away. He could get lost now.

4

He spent the afternoon on the public beach at Santa Monica. Beach kids all around him for safety. The report wrapped in his coat made a nice pillow. He might have caught a little nap, the rocking surf was soothing as a cradle.

He ate a good dinner in the canyon just off the beach. The next couple of hours he eliminated in a double-feature movie on Wilshire. When it was time to start for Hollywood, he took it easy.

There'd be a getaway car, he didn't have to park too near Mr. Oriole's. The old house looked quiet enough when he rolled by. But there were lights on behind the lace curtains and the shades were drawn. They were waiting for him.

He found a spot on a side street headed towards Sunset, left the car there. He walked back to Selma. The report was under his arm, the gun in the righthand pocket of his jacket. He didn't like to pack a gun but sometimes it was needed. When you were too rushed for a knife. He kept his fingers crossed that nothing had altered the schedule. He climbed the porch steps, hit the bell.

Mr. Oriole was a little cross. "So you are here."

"Who were you expecting?"

The door widened. "After last night, we did not know what to expect."

Steve walked in. "What are you grousing about?" His

voice was louder than it should be, to make sure it was heard in the next room. No sense going through the routine twice. "I was out working. You were sitting around on your fat behind."

Mr. Oriole's lip pouted but he only said, "In here," and parted the portieres.

The Eldon Moritzes weren't there or their lovely niece, they were too elegant for dirty business. But Schmidt was there, and Llewellyn, the bookshop fellow, already promoted to Albion's position? A burly six-footer who could drive piles with his bare fist was by the side window. His companion was the popcorn man. Steve wasn't surprised at the aggregation; this was it. The hatchet squad and the executives. First they'd have the report, then they'd hold court. Maybe Albion had passed on his suspicions. Maybe it was only Schmidt's jealousy. Easy enough to send black-bordered regrets to New York, accident in line of duty; better yet the outright lie that Stefan Winterich was a traitor. Even a suspected traitor didn't rate an investigation, much less a tear.

Steve took an arrogant stand, in line with the back-parlor exit. "Quite a gathering," he commented.

Schmidt was cold. But he couldn't quite disguise the crackle of excitement as his eyeglasses glinted towards the manuscript under Steve's arm. "You have the Davidian report?"

"Certainly I have it. You didn't think I'd be here wasting time if I didn't."

Schmidt's fingers trembled.

"The question is," Steve said insolently, "can you take care of it reaching New York safely?"

"You may depend on that." Schmidt's voice was almost eager.

Steve didn't pass it over yet. "I wasn't asked to bring it back. My part of the job ends right here."

"That is my understanding."

"Just so it's clear," Steve said. He walked over to Schmidt's chair. "It's your baby now." He let it drop to Schmidt's lap.

The neat fingers clutched it. The eyeglasses lifted after a moment. "You took care of Davidian?"

"What do you mean?"

From behind him he could feel the creak of the brute and the catarrhal breathing of the popcorn man. Mr. Oriole twined his plump hands together. Only Llewellyn, made in the Schmidt image, was unperturbed.

Schmidt almost screamed it. "You allowed him to escape?"

"He's around. All I did was get him drunk enough to talk. And take his God-damned report away from him."

Schmidt said thickly, "The F.B.I. will find him."

"They haven't."

"He can write another report." Schmidt was the type to worry. "He's a traitor. He can't be let go."

"I follow orders," Steve said. "That way I stay out of trouble. My orders didn't say anything about Davidian. Only to get the report." He moved as if he were about to leave. "I got the report. Okay?"

The scream was rising. "We don't know where he is."

Steve smiled. He swiveled his head to give all of them a good look at the smile. But he was getting nervy. It was time something should be happening. "You want me to bring him in?" The contempt for Schmidt's organization was as open as if he'd spit on them.

Schmidt was saved an answer. It began to happen. Steps on the porch, the doorbell. Mr. Oriole didn't believe it. He moved uncertainly in the direction of the disturbance. There was silence awaiting his return. It happened fast then. Schmidt clenching the report as Oriole returned with a big man; it was Hale. Ferber had come in the back way. There'd be others on the doors; a friend out back.

Hale said, "Federal Bureau of Investigation. Mr. Schmidt?"

Schmidt knew his rights. "I do not understand."

"We've got a few questions to ask you. And you, Mr. Oriole. And your Berlin friend, Steve Wintress, or Stefan Winterich."

Schmidt sputtered, "This is an outrage! You invade a private home—"

"We've got a warrant," Hale said patiently.

Ferber said, "I'll take those papers."

Schmidt hadn't known Ferber was behind him. He wasn't going to give up the report easy. They were both hanging onto the phony report. Steve dived as he announced, "I'm not taking this rap." Ferber was too busy to grab a gun. Oriole was in Hale's way. Steve dived for the back parlor, cracked out the window. He heard Hale's shout, Ferber's reassurance, "He can't get away." And a rumble, that would be Hale, "Where do you boys think you're going?" The goons wouldn't get to duck out.

And he was in the blackout of the back yard, cutting swiftly for the fence. A heavy hand on his shoulder halted him. "Come on."

156

He mouthed, "W-5," but the hold wasn't released. It couldn't be there'd be a mess-up now. There was no time for a confab, he had to get clear and fast.

He tried to wrest away but the clamp held on his shoulder. He didn't want to use the gun but it looked as if he'd have to. He was struggling for his pocket when the guy undertoned in his ear, "Come on, you fool! Why do you think the engine's running?"

He heard the purr of it then; recognized the shape of a car in the driveway headed towards the street. He let the fellow drag him along.

"Get in. Lie on the floor, pull the robe over you until we're out."

As Steve ducked into the rear, he caught a quick glimpse of the man. Wilton. He burrowed under the robe. Wilton was at the wheel and had the car rolling.

Steve told him, "I've got a car around the corner in the next block. Drop me there."

Wilton said, "You're driving this one."

A shapeless hat, an old raincoat. A man who was as much like him as his own brother. He should have caught on before. There were always earmarks of a man on a special assignment. He felt the swerve of the car out of the drive. They were picking up speed.

And then the implication of the words slashed through. He yanked the cover off his face. "I've got a bag and a hotel bill."

"They'll be handled."

He tried again, raising his voice enough for the weight of it to carry through. "I've got to make a stop."

"No stops."

"Look here, Wilton. It's safe. No one's looking for me tonight. The little Cocos won't move until Schmidt gives the word. And Schmidt's going to be too busy tonight to worry about me." It wouldn't take a minute. "The F.B.I. will know you've got me under wraps." Wilton could keep the car gunned while he picked her up.

"Orders, Steve."

Desperation tore the words from him. "I've got to, Wilton!"

She was there waiting for him, the pulse in her throat beating. He'd told her he'd come, that this time he wouldn't let anything keep him from coming.

"Sorry, Steve." Wilton meant it; he'd know; he was in the cage himself. "I've got to put you aboard a fishing smack at San Pedro before midnight. We're cutting it fine."

It wouldn't take a minute. Just while he told her it couldn't be tonight. The road from Hollywood to San Pedro wasn't by way of Main Street. *Some other time, baby.* It wouldn't take that long to look on her face once more.

"I signed you on two days ago. You'll find the duds I wore back on the seat. Once we get loose on Sepulveda you can change."

She'd wait for him until he didn't come. And then she'd walk home alone, hurting; hurting like hell tonight; tomorrow, hating.

"Your name is Dick Wilton. You'll get your new orders in LaPaz."

The punk in the sharp suit and the curly sideburns would want to take her home. She wouldn't let him tonight. At least tonight she'd walk alone.

"I drive the car over the border and ditch it. Your coat and hat will be in it and enough identification. You're getting away to Mexico." He made it clear. "We won't use you in this country again until it's safe." Until never. "Can't take any chances. You're worth too much to us, Steve."

The car was on a straightaway now, moving fast. Faster, further away from her waiting there. Her breasts rising and falling like proud music under the stars; her eyes watching every passer-by, eyes brighter than the brightest stars. Tomorrow they would be stones. If he could stop thinking about her . . . "How did the F.B.I. get into this?"

"We asked them in." There was relief in Wilton's voice. Steve was taking it. "We needed them. The C.I.C. hasn't any power in civvie matters. They get some men they've been watching; we get the report. Pop ought to be setting the real one down in Washington by now. No one will ever know the one you gave Schmidt was a phony. It'll be returned to us unread. Too bad, we coded a beaut. You can start changing, Steve. But keep down."

Don't take any chances. We need you. We need the bloody heart out of your body.

"How much does Haig know?"

"About you? Nothing. He knows our outfit loaned me to the F.B.I. to take Stefan Winterich. Unless he starts figuring. He's smart."

Smart enough to know that Steve was telling him that Janni might need help? Beyond the line of duty? Yeah, smart enough. Smart enough not to mention Steve, to let her forget, to take over.

158

"Conceited bastard."

"You're wrong. He's a straight shooter. He played it that way because of your reputation for arrogance, to beat you at your own game."

"He hates my guts."

"He hates the guts of anyone who's venal enough—or ignorant enough—to sell out to the Kremlin."

So he was a decent guy. So she'd be better off with him than she could ever have been with Stefan Winterich. Don't think about her. "What about Davidian?"

"He's safe."

"There isn't a safe place left," Steve said. "Nowhere in our world."

"That's why we're in this business," Wilton said.

Yes, that was why. The agents and the special agents of the Counter Intelligence Corps. Trained in—he could quote it word and letter— " . . . the art of catching spies, also the science of denying the enemy the information he must have . . ." The expendables. Eating danger and hanging onto the hope that men of good will would someday realize the old, old dream of peace. Until then there was the job, a dirty job, because war is dirty. You didn't need a proclamation calling it war; without peace, war was. Steve was a good agent, he could stoop to any dishonor without conscience, steal from a blind beggar, bribe a saint, lie to the beloved's face, murder without trace or tear. A monotone along the dusty alley of death.

Wilton said, "We think we can keep him safe. He's going to work for us."

"You can't trust him."

"We know. We've had others like him. But it's surprising how a man can change when he has plenty to eat and a decent place to live and a doctor to take care of the sore spots. When he's treated like a man. You can cure hate."

Steve had squirmed into the rough pants, the work shirt, the leather jacket. The suit he'd worn, this cloth her hands had touched, would disappear with Steve Wintress. And Davidian. She'd believe that he had hounded Davidian into another rotten exile.

"They'll catch up with him, Wilton." That hurt too. "They can't afford to let him go."

"Don't be so sure. We know a few tricks ourselves. He'll have you to dinner when you get back."

When you get back. If you get back. There's an end to everything, there's an end to this game. If only he could have told her. Who do you think held the gun at that guard's spine while Davidian scurried across the barrier? Who fixed it so that you could get away to the refuge of this last, very best hope of all men, this land still of the free and the brave? If only he could have touched her.

"You say something, Steve?"

"Nothing."

Some other time baby. Another year. Another eternity. *My darling . . . my darling . . .*

2

3
13 ◆   4

3
12 ✤   9

2
11 ◆   9

3
10 ◆   13

5
9 ✤   20

3
8 ◆   24

3
7 ✤   32

5
6 ◆   42

0
5 ♥   43

2
4 ✤   46

0
3 ✤   49

2
2 ♥   56

1 ◆   61

C

5
  9

6
  16

5
  27

5
  33

3
  35

2
  39

1
  42

2
  43

2
  47

1
  53

1
  53

0
  58

64